The Novelettes and Short Stories Are...
Cat Counting
The Monitor
Marketing
Over Here We Have
Chaos
Focus
Titles With Colons
Pigs and Other Living Things

# Over Here We Have

Sean Boling

Published by Sean Boling, 2024.

OVER HERE WE HAVE

**First edition. March 25, 2024.**



ISBN: 979-8224160143

Written by Sean Boling.

# Cat Counting
# (a novelette)

After my youngest brother and his wife had their youngest child, the cast of our family photo remained the same for about ten years. The kids grew up, my siblings and I aged, our parents shrunk, but the membership held steady for our celebrations that gave us a chance to line up and pose: kids sitting in front on the floor, siblings and spouses standing in the back, Mom and Dad in chairs in the middle.

Except for that one guy. There was always a random man standing in the back row, a different one in the same spot for each picture. He was my date, the latest prospect I brought to the latest party. My sibs would leaf through the photo albums Mom and Dad kept under the glass top of the coffee table in their living room and we would try to remember the names. I usually ended up as more of a judge, the game show host, rather than a participant, but sometimes I needed a minute to recall a name. My memory was not affected by how long ago I dated a particular subject, more so by how much hope I had for the relationship. The more fun I had with the man in the photo, the more I remembered his name. My siblings, particularly my brothers, had the opposite perspective. The bigger the stiff, the easier he was to make fun of, the more likely they were to remember his name. We played the game when I showed up without a date, or when the most recent guy was out of earshot for a while before dropping in on the middle of our conversation.

"Ricky," my older brother pointed to the photo of the man next to me I had brought to Dad's retirement party.

"No," my younger brother corrected him. "Just Rick."

"It was Ricky."

"No. You thought it was Ricky and he corrected you and said 'Just Rick.'"

"Poor guy corrected you about three times," my sister jumped into the debate.

"Just Rick," my younger brother imitated Rick, who was indeed a tight-ass that I only dated because I thought I was ready to settle.

"Way more than three times," I filled in some detail.

Recognition struck my older brother.

"I did it on purpose," he verbally slapped his forehead. "Rick."

This would be the point when my current date would show up after dutifully making conversation with my parents and ask "Who's Rick?"

But I had not brought a date for two consecutive family functions. I was in the process of making some personal changes, and thought a break from dating would enhance my focus.

They riffed some more on Rick, while I drifted into a sip from my wine glass and wondered if I had become "Just Bee" to any of the men I dated and their families, if I met them, if they remembered my name.

I remembered a party I attended with the man named Lamar. I thought it was one of those nights that predicted a bright future. It took place on the grounds of an old adobe ranch, the kind of place built by original Californios. Strands of lights fanned out from the top of a pole that rose from a three-tiered water fountain in the middle of the yard, each strand linked to one of the surrounding olive trees that lined an ancient wall. The conversations were easy. Wit and insight flowed between us and other guests, like the water that poured over the lips of the fountain in a soothing current. I felt so funny, so smart, had never felt more so. We made our way through a gate in the wall and discovered a pond on the other side, a reservoir that watered the cattle we had seen grazing on our drive in at sunset. The vineyards we could still make out in the moonlight below the ridgeline of the hills served as a stage for the night sky. Our lighting was perfect everywhere we went: the setting sun with its reassuring amber that seemed to light us from the inside, the candlelight glow of the bulbs strung over the courtyard, the moon and starlight casting us in a classic black and white film. I felt as beautiful as I did funny and smart. I remember those feelings even more than our kiss, and our kiss was perfect, a warm combination of ease and excitement.

I tried to find that house six months later.

I couldn't remember the way there, as I was too preoccupied with Lamar at the time. The hosts were friends of his, so I didn't know the address. I may have located it on a map, thanks to tracing several different routes and using satellite images to spot landmarks. I drove toward the likely candidate, but it lied at the end of a dusty road well beyond the city limits, where people can see you coming from a great distance. I didn't make it far enough down the road to see any trace of the house, if it was there. I felt more self-conscious the closer I may have been getting, and imagined being tongue-tied if someone asked me what I was doing out there on a road only driven by property owners, their guests, and delivery drivers. I was looking for more than the house, I could tell them. Maybe the grounds would tell me what went wrong after that perfect night. There was a clue I had missed. Maybe I wanted confirmation that the night even happened. I would arrive at the house and the owners would say we don't know anyone by that name, and we haven't thrown a party in years. Maybe seeing it in the daylight would tarnish the memory. I would see the rust and rot, the chipped edges and weeds, like the morning after an affair, but with a place rather than a person. I didn't need to see the house to try and make it mean something. I did that anyway, but none of my symbols held.

I stumbled upon a much more helpful metaphor one morning on my Sunday walk.

My route would remain the same for months, maybe years, until every so often I turned onto a random street to see what changed, and if the change was worth turning into my routine. Usually not much happened. The new street led to a familiar one soon enough, so even if I altered my course, the change was more of a tweak.

But the Sunday of my metaphor was a profound shift.

The street I chose had a bend, and beyond the bend was a dead end. I was about to turn around, but noticed an alley between two houses at the tip of the cul-de-sac. I walked through it and discovered a neighborhood I had never seen before.

A narrow park ran between two quiet streets with gentle parallel curves built into them. The winding greenbelt featured weeping willows every twenty yards, the needs of their deep roots met by a shallow trench of water that divided the grassy slopes. Humble tract houses lined one side of each street, facing the willowy greenbelt, and by extension facing each other. Each was a standard floor plan, the garage front-and-center, a front door and living room window squeezing into the frame, with so little space between the homes they could be mistaken for condominiums.

Variety flickered in what was planted in the front yards, and the color of each house. The color and trim also revealed that the row of houses on the south side of the park was thirty years older than the row on the north side. The older homes were beige, terra cotta, and brown. The heavy lifting of making the houses look unique was left to fake field stone plastered along the base and around the garage. If the style didn't betray their age, the rusty water stains cascading from leaks in the rain gutters did. Many of them had dried out front lawns, which are not unique to older homes, but the younger versions of themselves across the park that they faced had drought resistant front yards, with wood shavings, rocks, and plants that maintained their leaves and buds. The younger models were more colorful. Their blues, greens, yellows, and pinks provided enough character on their own without relying on fake rock trim.

I walked along the side of the park where the new houses stood, feeling as though I was caught between the past and the future. That wasn't the exact day I decided to take out a loan and finally wrap up my community college units and transfer to the nearest state university,

I had already started that process, but it represented my decision in a manner that would make a great point in one of my literature papers. Finding the reason I had never encountered this neighborhood before coiled the symbolism even tighter. The two streets were actually a single loop that led to a lone entrance, accessible on the edge of an industrial district that stretched behind the cement wall spanning the backyards of the younger houses. Its warehouses and factories filled the air with a hum that made the neighborhood feel like a simulacrum, as if the houses were a hologram designed to show potential buyers what their purchase may look like in thirty years, or what it used to look like thirty years ago.

Staring at my past, speculating on my future, feeling like my access points to a better outcome were dwindling, it all contributed to my excitement over getting started on my bachelor's degree.

I had never set foot on the campus until my first day of classes, it was simply the nearest option, so I felt a similar thrill of discovery on that first day as when I emerged from that dead end into a new neighborhood.

There was no ivy on the walls, no spires rising from brick buildings, it was every bit the state university, featuring lots of smooth concrete and oleander bushes. But I thought it was beautiful. The energy was the best part. Students were committed to a goal. So many in my community college classes had seemed unsure if they wanted to be there. Thanks to this shared sense of purpose at my new school, I didn't feel as old as I thought I would.

After that opening day, I wished I was taking all my classes on campus. Half of them were online. I designed it that way so I only had to drive the forty miles to campus twice a week, and keep my job at a reduced schedule the rest of the week in order to start making loan payments before I finished my degree. It seemed so sensible at the time I registered.

Then I checked in to my Social Ecology class, which was online, and any second thoughts I had about splitting my course load vanished. I ended up devouring so many of the modules during that first login, I was two weeks ahead when I at long last logged off. My scheduling decision turned out to be not only practical, but brilliant.

A bit lucky, too. I had done some research and found mostly positive reviews about the professor, Dr. Shea Dunn, but they were not effusive enough in their praise.

He produced a thrilling video for the opening module, which he narrated. He presents a man reading his online news feed, a harrowing series of stories convincing him the world is breaking down. Dr. Dunn's otherwise soothing baritone sounds ominous when set to images of communities at the breaking point, accompanied by the low hum of a synthesizer stalking the words and images, ready to crescendo. The man, whose face we never see, only pieces of him, rarely goes out. He works from home, has his groceries delivered, runs up and down the stairs for exercise, and is convinced that most everything beyond his garbage cans and mailbox is a threat to a quiet street like his. He arms himself, watches security camera videos of people firing their weapons during robberies and home invasions, and hits the pause button frequently as the host of the channel analyzes what the good guy with a gun did right and did wrong. When he takes a road trip to visit his sister, he straps a weapon to the side of the driver's seat near the parking break. As he drives along and stops occasionally, we as the audience see a normal world, but when the perspective shifts to his point of view, we see preludes to the next news item, constant cues to reach for the weapon. A minor incident happens, someone almost backs into his car as he exits a fast food restaurant parking lot, and he is far too ready be a hero in the next news cycle. The man in pieces rises from the driver's seat with his gun drawn.

The video cuts to darkness.

"Some in our field might call this the Availability Heuristic, others a Hasty Generalization, or Confirmation Bias," Dr. Dunn appears onscreen. "But by any name, it is one of the biggest obstacles to creating the kind of community that social ecologists dream of."

Dr. Dunn looked like a former leading man who made the transition to playing father figures, which kept me interested even as the production values shifted from the violent delusions of a spiraling man to a simple shot of the professor in his office talking to the camera. Maybe a younger set of eyes wouldn't find him as handsome. I couldn't compare my taste to that of the next generation, since there was no classroom full of them for me to survey, but I enjoyed being able to stare at him with no one there to tease me about gawking.

Regardless of whether they found him attractive, plenty of students on our first discussion board were wowed by the video.

"Wonder what the budget was," one of them typed. "Looks like the trailer for a legit movie."

"Not much," Dr. Dunn jumped in and replied. "I know some people."

He stayed out of our discussion threads for the most part. When he did post, he offered a compliment or a witty quip. He relied on chapters and articles scanned from a variety of books and journals that he posted on the website to impart most of the concepts which we wrote about and discussed, while inserting an occasional recorded video lecture of his own that was never more than five minutes. I appreciated the mystique he was cultivating, but would have preferred to see more of him. His comments on my work were professional and pointed where needed, but always contained more praise than criticism.

We were able to post a small picture of ourselves as part of our profile on the course website. I wavered between using a smiling or a serious shot, and whether to go with one that made me look younger or more accurate. My indecision rattled me. I feared my manic dating history was seeping into my new direction and undermining its purpose.

During my days of the week on campus, I bonded with a group of students who were in the traditional college age range. We had a standing reservation in one of the study rooms in the library. Our conversations often veered away from the subject we were studying, and I had something I wanted to ask the next time that happened.

"Anyone ever take Social Ecology with Dr. Dunn?"

"I did," said Mia.

I was glad one of the women said yes.

"He's all online, yeah?" said Mia's boyfriend, Trey.

"He is," I confirmed.

"Bleh," our study buddy Whitney chimed in. "My whole senior year was DE thanks to COVID. I'll never take another online course in my life."

"Well?" I asked Mia.

"He's fine," she shrugged.

"Fine, as in a decent teacher?" I probed.

Trey covered his mouth and laughed.

"What?" Mia reared back and glared at him.

Trey shook his head and stifled his laughter.

"Bee think Dr. Dunn a different kinda fine," Whitney answered on behalf of Trey.

Rather than deny my crush, I owned it. I needed to. It was my only chance for a breakthrough. And the kids were having so much fun.

"Am I seeing things?" I asked Mia.

"I can see it," she tried to remember him. "I guess."

"If you were older," I completed her thought.

"Well, yeah."

They had even more fun. I thought a librarian was going to rap on the glass of our study room window, but the glass, or maybe the librarians, were thick enough to let us roll. I confessed my concern over whether my motivation was being seized by desperation.

"Everyone's looking for someone," Whitney assured me. "You don't turn that off just 'cause you're going to college."

"Look at us," Trey put his arm around Mia.

I smiled at them.

"You could say something right now," Mia grinned back. "Couldn't you?"

"I won't," I held up my hand as if taking an oath. "I don't want to be jaded. Not here. I've got the other days of the week for that."

I relied on our study sessions to air all of my feelings about going to college full-time, not just my feelings for Dr. Dunn.

I avoided talking about my education while at work. Sometimes I had to bring it up with management in order to arrange my schedule. They already had their degrees, and the encouragement they provided always felt condescending, as though they thought it was cute that I was earning mine, but that school can only take you so far, and it takes a special person to operate a wholesale truck engine parts distribution center. My co-workers were the opposite. They saw my education as something I was holding over them, a way for me to feel superior, so I never brought it up in their company.

As the semester drew down to its last couple of weeks, I took my study buddies out for lunch to thank them for the camaraderie they provided. The campus food court wasn't enough to express my gratitude, so I sprung for a trendy spot downtown. It was a late lunch, after we were done with classes for the day, and the bar was populated by a well-dressed horde who snuck out of work early to get a head start on happy hour.

Whitney had been to that kind of place before, and Trey worked at one. Mia was a bit wide-eyed, but settled in soon enough. By the time our food arrived, we were sharing stories and throwing barbs as if we were in our study room at the library. Instead of a librarian tapping on the window, I thought maybe our server or the manager would ask us to quiet down, but we were barely keeping up with the clamor of relieved people happy to be out of the office.

With the four of us doing our part in contributing to the commotion, I had no chance of camouflaging my reaction when I saw Dr. Dunn at the bar. Two seconds of silence and stillness while staring at a fixed point was all it took for them to notice I had been jerked from the moment. Mia and Whitney asked me what was up, while Trey tracked my gaze to see if he could see what I was seeing. There were far too many people at the bar for him to figure out which one froze me, and he didn't know what Dr. Dunn looked like, so I was able to dodge my discovery with an excuse about thinking I saw an old boyfriend. I didn't want them to know I spotted Dunn. I wanted to approach him without a cheering section, so I kept an eye on him as we finished our meal.

Pretending not to keep an eye on him was distracting. I felt guilty for not giving my classmates my full attention, guilt that I paid off when the check came and they thanked me several times each. Rather than make up an excuse to stay, I left with them and waited for an opportunity to walk back to the restaurant. I was hoping they would all head in the same direction, but Trey and Mia went one way, and Whitney the other. I went with Trey and Mia, figuring they would be too involved with each other to notice anything I did that was not sneaky enough.

After we passed the first cross street and they didn't turn, I pretended to realize I had parked down that street and made fun of myself for being such a ditz. They each gave me a hug. When they walked away, I took a few steps down the decoy street, lingered half-hidden by the building on the corner, then waited until they reached the end of the block before walking back to the happy hour featuring Dr. Dunn.

He was talking to a woman at the bar who wasn't with him earlier. They were too busy trying to make each other laugh to be in a relationship. This was good news, unless he was cheating on someone. I ordered a glass of sauvignon blanc to steady my nerves without staining my teeth, and waited for her to use the restroom.

Night fell outside, the lights took hold inside. She was relentless. Neither toilet nor mirror could pull her away from Dr. Dunn. I understood, but was annoyed nonetheless. He finally asked to close his tab and she still had yet to surrender her seat. Before he could offer to pay hers, I moved in.

"Dr. Dunn?" I asked for confirmation. "Social Ecology?"

He treated my question like an accusation that he tried to laugh off.

The woman wanted an answer more than I did.

"I told Shea this would happen," he said more to himself than either of us.

"There's another Shea?" I asked.

"Who's Shea?" the woman asked.

"An old friend of mine," he answered her as if I wasn't there. "She's a professor at State. Teaches online."

He looked at me.

"I helped her produce some videos for her class," he invited me back into the conversation.

"Starring you as her," I put the pieces together.

"I never actually say that I'm her," he clarified. "I introduce the class and discuss some concepts, but I never say her name."

"It's strongly implied."

"And legally permissible."

I needed a moment to sift through all I had learned in the last ten seconds.

"Why does she do this?" I asked.

"I don't want to speak for her," he studied his empty beer glass. "But she told me it has to do with respect. Respect she felt she wasn't getting as a woman professor."

"She used to teach in person?"

"For quite a while," he nodded. "Fifteen, twenty years? That's why when she first went online, her classes were all text, no videos. She had to disappear for a couple years so that any student who took her in person would be gone by the time she re-emerged in her new form."

"New form," I scoffed.

"I'm Clark," he extended his hand. "I run a small production company. Local commercials mostly."

"Mostly," I waved rather than accept his handshake.

The woman appreciated my gesture. We looked at one another and formed a brief sisterhood.

"I understand," Clark broke us up. "You're disappointed. Maybe feeling betrayed? I don't want to read too much into your reaction any more than I want to speak for Shea. But if you take this up with her, please do it in a private message. Don't out her on the site."

"The class is almost over, and I've got a strong 'A'. I'm not risking that."

Clark laughed.

I understood why, but I had waited too long to finish my degree. I could see the woman was on my side. I wondered if she was a date, or if he had met her there.

"There is another way," he said as he settled down.

"Another way to what?"

"Get to know her, reach out, whatever you decide to do, if anything."

"Really?" I prompted him.

"She has a YouTube channel with a lot of audience interaction."

"As herself?"

"She goes by 'Shea'," he answered. "No Doctor, no last name."

"Only one keyword. That makes it hard to find."

"It's called Cat Walk," he stood up and laid enough cash over the tab to cover all of us. "Enjoy."

I apologized to the woman for interrupting their evening.

"You added another layer," she said.

"We should hang out sometime," I said to her.

Clark was a good sport. He smiled at me as he took her by the hand and they worked their way out.

Shea's channel was actually called "Cat Counting". I thought Cat Walk was a better name. I wondered if Clark suggested it, Shea rejected it, and he continued to refer to it as Cat Walk to annoy her. He seemed like the kind of person who found humor in annoying people.

I enjoyed seeing the real her, but didn't find the premise of the series very interesting based on the first video I watched. I was too caught up in studying her appearance and her voice to find the idea of counting the cats she saw on her morning walk as anything other than a waste of time. She had over four thousand subscribers, though, and the latest video she had posted, which was my introduction to the collection, had surpassed a thousand views over its first two days, so I gave it a chance by following her orders in the description below the video that read, "New to Cat Counting? Please watch our Orientation". The word "Orientation" was hyperlinked to a video called "Welcome to Cat Counting".

She didn't just walk through her neighborhood and count cats. She approached the process as though teaching a class, only this version was low-tech, spontaneous, and dealt with a topic that was not at all important.

I fell in love with her work all over again.

"I walked this route for seven months before I decided it might be fun to start documenting the stories that take place in its windows, front yards, vacant lots, parklands, and under its parked cars," she said while standing in front of a closed door that I assumed was the entrance to her house. "Before I introduce you to our setting and maybe a few of the characters if they're out and about—I'm recording this a little later in the morning than usual for some brighter light, so that means most of our stars have already retired for the day after being out all night—I wanted to share a few fun facts. On one of my walks before I started to film, I took note of every spot where I recalled seeing a cat, and added them up for a total number of possible sightings, as if all of them happened to be visible on a single walk, and came up with just over one hundred cats. I was delighted to arrive at that number, because it made the math easy. My average number of sightings is twenty-one per walk, which led me to my hypothesis that we only see about twenty percent of the cats that are actually around us when we're out in the world, or at least in a world like this neighborhood. Three of my regulars let me pet them, and I've encountered a few more sporadic cats who let me pet them, so we can estimate that around five percent of cats are friendly. Again, that number may vary depending on the environment, but that seems about right across the board, don't you think? Let me know in the comments section."

She reached toward the camera to turn it off, then thought of something.

"My record for a single walk is twenty-nine," she smiled. "Maybe someday we can beat that. Together."

Her image jiggled in stride as she walked while holding the camera selfie-style during her next riff.

"Sometimes you're going to have to take my word for it that I've spotted one," her voice was a bit breathy from walking and talking at the same time. "I don't aim my camera at a cat if there's a person nearby, or if there's a cat in a window. Like Red Bones, the little orange guy who stares out the front window of a house with rusty camper shells stacked in the driveway and an Oath Keepers yard sign stuck in the weeds. I am not pointing my camera at that property. It might be the last thing I ever do, and I'm sure they'd bury my phone with me to hide the evidence."

"That's Stumpy Gray," she whispered in the background of her next shot, a steady zoom on a portly gray tabby with short legs glaring at her on all fours from under a trampoline in a front yard. "At least that's what I call him. I only know the real names of two cats, a couple of friendlies with collars that I don't see very often. Stumpy's not exactly a regular, but not a rare sighting, either. There are three kinds of cats on my route. The reliable ones I can count on seeing nearly every day, the sporadic cats who come and go, and the legends. I'm lucky to see a legend once a month. Some legends I've only seen once, maybe twice, in the seven months I've spent walking this timeline. I'm starting wonder if I ever really saw them."

Stumpy Gray assumed a sitting position and started to lick his front paw, trying to prove he didn't care that he had been spotted. Shea widened the shot and Stumpy became a smaller part of the landscape. I noticed the trampoline was slightly askew, tilting along with the slope of the yard. I imagined children bouncing on it, drifting gradually to the edge, then being catapulted onto the dirt where the lawn once was.

She cut to a shot of a sidewalk ahead of her as she walked along. The neighborhood was more upscale than in the previous cuts.

"We walk through a variety of settings on our route. There are two neighborhoods that have seen better days. How much better, I can't say. Two other neighborhoods are tract home developments. Nice, but indistinguishable. And one, this one, is visibly wealthy."

She turned the camera back onto herself as she continued to walk.

"The neighborhoods don't seem to influence the cats' behavior much. Having a house and someone who feeds them appears to be a great stabilizer. Being stray applies the greatest pressure. A cat in a neighborhood may not come to you when you squat down and try to lure them over by slowly blinking your eyes and speaking to them gently, but they'll at least look at you. A cat in a vacant lot or park will run away the moment you start to squat. Something else I've noticed about the neighborhoods is that the rugged homes and the opulent ones have most of the cats. The middle of the road homes, the tract homes, don't seem to have as many cats. I have some ideas why that may be, but I'd prefer to hear yours in the comment thread before I share mine."

I scrolled through the comments to see what ideas her audience had generated, but it had been too long since she asked the question, and whatever answers they shared were buried deep in the comments posted since. If I was disappointed, the feeling didn't last long, because I was so struck by the tone of the comment thread.

It was what the web can be, what its founders imagined it would be, full of people on board ready to learn about others rather than defeat them. The most recent series of posts was a confessional, a long line of cat hoarders admitting how many they harbored, and why. The numbers were alarming, but the explanations kept me reading.

Most acknowledged the cats were filling holes drilled by people who were supposed to love them but didn't, or loved ones who left, by choice or by death, or that the holes were already there because there were no loved ones to begin with. Others insisted they were growing their cat population simply because they found them "beautiful", or "fascinating", or some other vague adjective. Their fellow community members did not let them hide behind words that could describe anything and explained nothing. But they didn't accuse them of hiding. Instead they asked questions. They asked when their collection started, or who inspired their obsession.

Dr. Dunn asked the best questions of all thanks to her professorial instincts. She moderated the conversation, while probing for greater detail. She asked one woman to describe the house where she and the cats lived, which led to a history of who owned it, which led to the story of her inheritance. Her husband wrangled the property away from her siblings, which led to estrangement from her family, which led to a divorce, then seclusion, and eventually more cats on the property, thirty-two, than Dr. Dunn saw on her most successful day of cat counting, which as far as I knew was still twenty-nine.

I was surprised that no one guessed what Shea did for a living, or tried to, in the comments I read. But then nobody referenced anything about their life that wasn't tethered to an interest in cats. They left everything else behind when they visited her channel.

She posted one video per week. Usually it was a collection of highlights from that week's walks, but if one walk in particular was noteworthy, thanks to nearly setting a new record, seeing a legend or two, or encountering every friendly along the way, she posted the highlights of that specific journey.

I got to know the cats, and like other fans of the channel, developed some favorites. My favorite regular was big, old, reliable Clippy, a calico with the top of her right ear missing who sat in front of a house that had Halloween decorations on the front lawn year-round. I liked to think the owners kept the decorations up because they worked so well with the Clippy's orange and black markings. My favorites from the sporadic category were the Boat Boys. They were three cats whose black-and-white markings made them look like they were wearing tuxedos as they lounged on top of a speed boat that was parked in their driveway. At least one of them was usually there, but they only appeared together about once every two weeks, and they never looked at Shea, no matter how sweet or how distracting she tried to be. My favorite legend was a cat she dubbed The Galoot. It would materialize every couple of months in a vacant lot, and she had never seen the whole cat, only its massive head looming above the weeds. It appeared to be a well-groomed Siamese, so Shea speculated it was a spoiled indoor cat that escaped every so often not to taste freedom, but to scare its owners into doting on it even more.

I spent most of my semester break binge-watching her channel. The degree plan I worked on with my counselor didn't provide space for any more of her classes if I wanted to finish within my budget, so I was grateful for the chance to stay connected with her. The fact it was really her, not her academic silhouette, made the channel more appealing than her class, anyway.

The growing academic in me, though, questioned the idea that it was really her. It was still a video representation of her. She controlled her persona, selected what we could see. We didn't know her from watching her, we only thought we did.

I re-watched the whole series, looking for clues that revealed where she took her walk. I paused on frames that included street signs in the background, screen-captured them, zoomed in on the names, and sharpened the focus. I jotted down the numbers on the houses, assumed they were in the same city as the university, typed the addresses into an online satellite map, and looked for certain boats in driveways and Halloween decorations in front yards.

Her route was eleven miles away from campus.

I had already scheduled my on-campus classes for spring semester to start late in the morning to allow plenty of time for my commute. I wouldn't even need to bring a change of clothes. Stretch pants, a pullover, and sneakers would further assimilate me into the college aesthetic. All I had to do was leave earlier. Based on the position of the sun in her shots, she walked within an hour after sunrise.

Touring her route was like visiting the set of a production. I even parked a couple of blocks away, as if the neighborhoods where she pointed her camera phone were part of a studio backlot that I needed to enter from the outside. Spotting the cats in person was like lining up alongside the red carpet at a movie premiere. I waved at each cast member and tingled with excitement when one of them looked at me. I even met one of the friendlies, an orange tomcat who liked to roll around on the sidewalk for belly rubs. Dr. Dunn called him Frank.

I eventually met Dr. Dunn, too, but it took three weeks.

Part of the delay was a matter of time, as I couldn't know exactly when she was on the move, and the other part was a matter of space, as I didn't know exactly where the route ran, only specific streets, and I took many wrong turns during those first several walks.

When I did finally see her, it was from a distance. I turned onto a street that sloped upward and saw her two blocks ahead of me, at the top where the sidewalk crested, aiming her phone at something across the street, holding a pose in profile that made her look like a statue dedicated to her work as a cat counter.

I stopped and appreciated the image, as though at a national park or museum. When she finished shooting and walked on, I accelerated my stride so as not to lose her trail. I caught sight of her again when I reached the bluff where her temporary monument had been, and slackened my pace so I stopped looking like a racewalker and more like someone out for a leisurely stroll. I wasn't prepared to speak with her, I grew flustered at the thought of it, so I simply followed her home, passed by her house, and identified a good place to park for my next visit.

I arrived around sunrise. I only had to wait in my car for half an hour before she emerged from her house. She headed in the same direction as she walked last time, as though picking up where she left off, which meant her route was a winding loop, starting on one side of the walkway that led to her door, and ending on the other. I jumped out of my car and headed in the opposite direction, so I could start connecting with her by waving and smiling as our paths crossed.

We also said "good morning".

For two more weeks, four sessions' worth of walks, we smiled and waved and said "good morning" as we passed by each other. The first three crossings happened when she was between cat sightings, she was simply walking, phone in her pocket. The fourth time she was aiming her phone at Blinky, a sporadic Abyssinian who liked to nap under a window box full of flowers in the ritzy neighborhood, but was also a light sleeper who sensed Shea's presence no matter how quiet she was, and always woke up annoyed and blinking. I wanted to drop some knowledge about Blinky, to signal my fandom, but thought that might be jarring, so I tried to think of something else to say as I approached the scene. Shea holstered her phone and started walking in my direction before I found the words, so all I said was "Good morning."

I was not going to let that happen again.

The following walk, she was once more between shots as we approached each other on a lengthy stretch of sidewalk that lined a wall surrounding one of the housing tracts. It was a section of the route she referred to in a few episodes as a "no cat zone". She sometimes used it as a backdrop for when she wanted to address the camera while in motion, and had only ever seen one cat perched on the wall, a Russian Blue legend captured but twice on video. She wasn't talking to her camera on that fifth day, so I had my chance.

"You must have just moved here," she beat me to it.

"Oh..." I tried to think of a response since I could no longer use my prepared statement.

"Or you just took up walking," she said in passing.

She was getting away.

"I'm a big fan," I blurted out.

She stopped and turned to face me.

"Of Cat Counting?"

"Of course," I said. "I love it. Those cats are like the cast of *Friends* as far as I'm concerned."

"Huh," she looked away and looked perplexed.

"I guess I should go with a reality show for my analogy," I started to get comfortable. "Like they're the cast of *Real Housewives of Orange County*. Or wherever. Maybe you should have called it *Real Housecats of...*"

"But you do live here," she trained her attention back on me.

"Well..." my comfort collapsed.

"How did you find the neighborhood?"

"Um..."

"That took a lot of work."

"It all started when I took a class from you," I said, thinking the academic connection would make me sound less crazed, but realized it further burnished my stalker profile.

"Wait a second," she moved towards me. "Did you meet Clark not too long ago? In a bar?"

"Yes," I admitted, not sure how it would play, but not prepared to lie.

"Ah..." her relief rubbed off on me.

"That was me," I held out my arms as if being introduced to a crowd.

"Okay, this makes more sense now."

"You've never been approached by a fan?"

"Not in person," she said. "No."

"You have thousands of them."

"You've obviously spent time on the web."

"Obviously."

"And you visit other websites besides mine."

"Yes."

"Then you have to know what a paltry number that is."

"It's still five thousand people. That would look impressive if they were all in one place."

"Out of hundreds of millions of people in the country, billions in the world. And what are the odds any of them live here, or lived here before? Even if they recognized the neighborhood, who would go to all that effort to track me down?"

"Well, if they really liked your channel..."

I tried not to sound embarrassed.

"I'm sorry," she put her hand to her forehead. "This is no way to treat a fan. I assume."

"Think of me as a student," I suggested. "Not the kind that drove you to Distance Ed. The kind of student you liked. You must have liked some of them."

She laughed.

"Of course I did," she said. "I think."

I volleyed back some laughter of my own.

"What's your name?" she asked. "I don't think Clark told me."

"I never told him."

"Smart."

"He was with some woman. I think they just met that night."

"Lucky. For you, I mean."

"My name is Bee. I spell it like a honeybee. Short for Beatrice, so it should be B-e-a, but I don't like either my full name or the traditional short version."

"I remember that name from last semester."

"Really?"

"Social Ecology 202, right?"

"That's why I spell it that way."

"It's not just the spelling. You were good. Really good."

I was honored.

"Thank you," I managed to say before my voice quivered.

She gestured for me to join her.

"I've got coffee brewing at the house."

"Oh, really, you don't have to..."

"I want to."

"Honestly..."

"Please. I insist. You wanted to meet me, right?"

"Well, yes."

"You didn't just want to say hello."

"I hadn't really thought of what would happen after that."

"This is what's happening," she grabbed my arm and started walking. "Let's go. Before the cats check out for the day. I need more footage."

"Okay," I beamed. "But I have a class at eleven."

"How long were you expecting to stay?" she let go of my arm.

"I don't..."

She smiled to let me know she was teasing.

I stopped talking and we walked side by side.

I didn't worry about not knowing what to say, or being self-conscious about saying whatever came to mind. We would come to the end of the no-cat-zone wall, we would encounter some characters, and that would give us plenty to talk about. But the wall was much longer in person than it came across on screen, and my discomfort grew in stride with its length. I finally saw a street ahead of us I assumed marked our turn back into cat country, but the distance created more silence than I could stand.

"I think I know why there aren't many cats in the middle-class housing tracts," I said.

"Okay," she was perplexed, but was nice enough not to say what-are-you-talking-about.

"You asked that question in your orientation video."

"Oh," she remembered. "Right. That one didn't generate a lot of responses. People like to talk about themselves, but they don't like to talk about how much money they have, at least not honestly, so that prompt really put them in the spin cycle. Walked right past it, whistling a made-up tune, avoiding eye contact."

Our silence put itself back together over our next several steps. I wished I had gone with something else to break it.

"So..." she said.

"What?"

"The reason there aren't many cats in the tracts."

"Ah," I longed for the quiet of five seconds earlier.

"Just because my prompt was a bomb doesn't mean there aren't good answers to it."

The unintentional buildup added more pressure. I concentrated on my words so I wouldn't sound as though I was blurting them out.

"Because of how much the middle class fusses over nice things."

"I like where you're going with this," she encouraged me.

"The struggling class doesn't have those things, so they don't worry about what a cat might do to them. The upper class can clean or replace stuff a cat gets into, so they don't worry about them either. The middle class can afford stuff, but it's a bigger slice of their pie, so they fret over what they buy. A cat is a risk on their investment."

"Bonus points for not using the term 'bourgeoisie values,'" she cracked.

We passed the wall and turned the corner, entering one of the tract developments in question.

"I remember liking that about your writing," she added. "You're good at avoiding jargon, and coming up with clear ways of expressing yourself, instead of trying to impress the teacher."

"Thank you."

She stopped in her tracks, holding her arm out in front of me, as though driving a car and suddenly having to apply the brakes with a loved one in the passenger seat.

"Look at that," she stared ahead of us.

I was too busy considering her arm gesture, and infusing it with meaning, to notice what she was looking at.

"You posit your theory on the relationship between the middle class and their lack of cats, and presto, a cat immediately appears as soon as we set foot in their neighborhood."

I saw Triple T crossing the sidewalk two doors down our path. She was a small tortoiseshell cat whose full name was Teeny Tiny Tortie.

"Triple T says, *'Not so fast, I beg to differ,'*" Shea projected her thoughts onto her. "*'Case in point: me!'*"

"It's not an absolute," I jumped in. "Just a trend."

"Actually," Shea moved her hand onto my shoulder. "Your theory..."

"More of a hypothesis," I corrected her. "Maybe just an idea."

"...it may still stand," she ignored my equivocations and proceeded forward.

I followed and we stopped in front of Teeny Tiny Tortie's house as she flopped on the dry front lawn and stared at us.

"Listen," she said quietly.

"You're not going to get any shots of her? She's a sporadic."

"Not now," she said. "Listen."

We stood there a long time.

Long enough to feel odd.

Shea devised a plan.

"I'm going to pretend to talk to you, and you pretend to listen," she said as quietly as she could without whispering. "But what you're really listening for is a sound coming from the house."

She started the ruse, moving her mouth without saying anything, and gesturing with her hands to enhance the effect.

"Did you hear it?" she snuck in words at one point.

"Hear what?" I asked.

"Try again," she said. "It takes about thirty seconds."

She went back to miming a conversation.

This time I heard it: a small beep, barely perceptible, from inside the house.

"Recognize that noise?" she asked.

"A smoke alarm with a dead battery."

"Correct."

It was my turn to be perplexed. I awaited further explanation.

"Two years," she said.

"Seriously?"

She nodded and signaled for us to start walking.

After we passed the house next door to the one with the smoke alarm that had been signaling it had a dead battery for two years, she spoke at normal volume.

"The entire time I've been walking this route. So who knows how long before that."

"That's nuts."

"Perhaps. But the point is I don't think they're middle class. They're renting in a middle-class neighborhood, or they moved up beyond their means. So Triple T doesn't refute your idea, she confirms it."

I was more interested in how she noticed the faint beep from inside the house in the first place.

"The first time I saw Tortie I tried to woo her," she explained. "As usual, with any cat, so I crouched down on the sidewalk and realized pretty quickly she was quite the bitch, but thought I heard the beep, and stayed down in the crouch to confirm it. I didn't think anything of it, smoke alarm batteries die all the time, but happened to hear it the next time I made a futile attempt to seduce her, and ever since."

"I'll bet you could make some great episodes about the houses on your route."

"I could," she agreed. "And I thought about it."

She pointed at the second story window of a house we were passing.

"Those blinds have been tilted at the same angle for as long as the smoke alarm has been dead. Then there's the house coming up in the next neighborhood that's obsessed with dog shit."

"How can you tell?"

"Three different signs: one standard 'pick up after your dog' version; another one trying to be funny, something about shit happens, only they use the word 'poop'; and then a warning on a rock, like it's a commandment, which I guess is also supposed to be funny. You'll see. You can be the judge."

"Why don't you?"

"I don't care enough. I can't even remember the exact wording of the signs and I walk by them every day."

"No, I mean, why don't you shoot the house episodes?"

"I'm not interested in humiliating people," she said as we took our latest turn. "Even if I was careful to just focus on the thing I was goofing on, and not reveal any addresses, I'd be yet another person on the web being snarky about another person. Not what the world needs."

Her concern with respect for others made me wonder about her departure from live teaching. I considered using the moment to ask what it was that drove her away, but she wasn't finished.

"I'm also certain I'd discover that something I made fun of had a very sad backstory. Like the reason the weed whacker has been in the driveway of that house on Mariposa Street for five months is because a widow's husband laid it there right before he had a heart attack, and she can't bring herself to move it, and won't let anyone move it, either."

"That weed whacker is in a few shots, isn't it?"

"Gordon Fluffybutt lives there," she confirmed.

"That's right," I gasped. "I love Gordon."

"Everyone loves Gordon," she brushed past my excitement to make a final point about houses. "And above all else, I am hardly one to talk about household quirks."

"None of us are."

"'Quirks' is putting it far too mildly," she said. "You'll see."

She was referring to the people inside her house rather than the house itself, for it was as immaculate inside as it was outside.

"I wouldn't be able to afford this if I got my job today," she said as she dropped her keys in a bowl on a table inside the front door. "But twenty-five years ago it was in my range. Timing. Life is mostly luck."

She closed the door behind me.

"Hello!" she called out.

"Hello!" a woman's voice called back.

"We have company!"

"Anyone I know?"

"You have no friends!"

"An acquaintance? One of our weird neighbors?"

We walked toward the voice until we found its source in a kitchen nook sitting in front of a laptop and an oversized coffee mug. The light shining through the windows behind her bounced off the white furniture and walls to an almost blinding degree. She looked like she was having coffee in heaven, or on the set of a Pottery Barn photo shoot.

Shea squeezed around the nook table and leaned over for a kiss.

"Eee-ooh," she said.

"Eee-ooh," her partner answered back when their peck was complete.

Shea looked over at me while she was still bent over next to her.

"That's what it sounded like the first time she farted in front of me," she said.

"A major milestone," her partner reminisced. "First fart."

"I'm sorry," Shea chuckled as she stood up straight and headed for the coffee maker and the mugs in the cupboard above it. "We've been working from home for so long we have no boundaries anymore and no social grace."

"Speak for yourself. I'm simply at a point in life where I don't care what people think. We've talked about this."

"I'm Bee," I tried to normalize the conversation.

"Oh. Of course. I'm Nora," she respected my play.

"A former student," Shea prepared our coffees.

"Wow," said Nora. "What a throwback. It's been years since I've met one of your students. It's been years since you've met one of your students."

"Are you a professor, too?" I asked Nora.

"I'm a Data Analyst," she said.

"Oh," I thought that sounded interesting, since it's the kind of thing we did in some of my classes, but I was afraid my 'oh' didn't communicate that enthusiasm.

"You're not going to tell her whose data you analyze?" Shea brought me a cup of coffee in one of their large mugs that required two hands to hold it.

"A large, awful company that poisons water and pollutes the air. Is that what you want me to say?"

"She used to be an Institutional Research Analyst for our school," Shea told me. "Doesn't Institutional Research sound more dignified than Data Analyst?"

"Doesn't Data Analyst sound like it pays more?" Nora checked an alert that pinged on her screen, then disregarded it. "How did you manage to meet a student, if I may change the subject?"

I wasn't sure where to begin, so Shea took the lead.

"She took Social Ecology and ran into Clark at a bar."

"Did he hit on you?"

"He was already hitting on someone," I answered.

"Like that matters," Nora said. "Did he pretend to be your professor for as long as he could?"

"I guess we've found the one thing that can knock him off his game," Shea said before sipping her coffee.

"He'll be prepared next time," Nora scoffed, then closed her laptop. "You seem a little older than your average college student. What's your story?"

Shea groaned with embarrassment.

"You couldn't just ask 'what's your story'?"

Nora raised her palms in a defensive shrug.

"A late bloomer," I answered her question to keep the peace. "I finally started taking high school seriously my senior year, thanks to a couple of great teachers. By then it was too late. I wasn't on the college track. I went to community college but was seduced by a job that paid well for someone my age, so I dropped out and worked. The pay didn't seem so great once I wasn't that age anymore, and I kept thinking about school, and what could have been if I had those teachers earlier. So I went back, took about seven years to transfer, and here I am."

"And that's why you don't teach at some snooty private college, right hon?" Nora stood and approached us. "You wouldn't have these wonderful students like Bee in your class."

She kissed Shea, then reached out and grabbed my forearm.

"You were my favorite category when I worked in IR at the university."

Shea groaned again.

"I get it," I assured her. "Thank you, Nora."

"She gets it," Nora gestured my way while nodding at Shea.

Shea kept one hand on her mug while pretending to fling her coffee at Nora with the other.

Maybe their behavior around me was a performance and their private life was very different than the one I was allowed to see, but they truly did seem to think that roasting each other made their relationship more delicious.

We started a routine where I caught their act once a week before class, after Shea finished her walk. The show included breakfast in their luminous nook, a first look at the unedited footage from that week's walks, and a feeling I had arrived at the place I hoped to reach when I started going to college.

Attending classes built social credit that I spent on time with Shea and Nora, while the ways I previously spent my time started to recede. My job was even more enjoyable than when I first started, now that I could see it ending in the near future. My study buddies were still a pleasant diversion from studying, but when I was with Shea and Nora, I was the young one, a protégé rather than a mentor, and I didn't feel qualified to be any sort of mentor, much less a sage, to people younger than me.

I started to meet Shea and Nora for dinner on occasional weekends. They treated me to restaurants that didn't have any televisions tuned to sporting events, where the servers were professional rather than college students, and decisions on what to order required reading the menu analytically since the dishes were unique to the chef.

The conversations were the same as the ones I had at bars and grills and fast food restaurants. We discussed why we like some things and don't like others, only the areas of expertise were different. Instead of talking about whether the Forty-Niners or Seahawks were going to make it to the Super Bowl, we talked about whether Hegel or Burke had the answers to our modern problems. Instead of explaining why we liked a movie, we explained why we liked an independent film. And we talked about relationships, like anyone else, about friends and colleagues and lovers.

They were fascinated by my dating history, so much so that Shea apologized one night for their fixation.

"We've been together so long, and were in such lengthy relationships before we met, your story is grand opera," she said.

The three of us were at a corner table in a new tavern that labeled itself a speakeasy, sharing a bottle of Syrah because the cocktail menu was so long and bewildering that none of us could decide on drinks of our own.

"I always feel like we're around a campfire when you tell us about your dates," Nora added.

"Because they're so scary?" I asked.

"Yes," she liked that reason. "Yes. They frighten me."

She looked at Shea.

They appeared to have planned something.

Shea nodded for Nora to proceed.

"Scary, scary," she hedged. "Scary indeed. Which is why we want to set you up with someone."

"Clark?" I asked.

"You already have plenty of stories to tell," said Shea. "With a lot of Clarks in them."

"It's about time for a relationship that doesn't generate a lot of stories," added Nora. "Just contentment. When someone asks how it's going, you simply say 'fine.'"

"And you have someone like that in mind for me," I confirmed. "Someone dull."

"He's not exactly dull," Nora said.

"He's pretty close," Shea said into her glass as she raised it to her lips.

"He's quiet," Nora insisted.

"He's her son," Shea revealed upon completing her sip.

"You have a son?" I asked Nora.

"From my previous marriage," she decided it was time for a sip of her own.

"I was pretty good at lying to myself," Shea mused. "She was awesome at it."

"His name is Ram," Nora proceeded.

"And his name is the most interesting thing about him," Shea tried to land another jab, but Nora didn't flinch.

"Nonsense," she snapped back. "He has great hair."

"That's not interesting," Shea considered her point. "He dresses well. That's more along the lines of interesting."

"That's our motto," Nora sighed. "Great hair. Dresses with flair. Not much there."

"And by 'our,'" Shea clarified, "she means us, not she and her ex-husband."

"He would never say that about him," Nora said. "They're too much alike."

"Is Ram short for Ramses, as in the Egyptian pharaoh?" I asked. "Or Ramsey. As in Ramsey."

"His father wanted it to be Ramses."

"He's a Doctor of Ancient Civilizations," Shea chipped in.

"I told him it would be confusing at best, requiring constant corrections on how to spell it, and at worst, be a tribute to entitlement and abuse of power."

"So it's Ramsey," I confirmed.

"We just went with Ram," Nora shrugged. "Kept it short. Or as his father put it, created a mystery."

Shea giggled.

"What?" I asked.

"An unsolvable mystery," she said.

"That sounds kind of alluring," I perked up.

"Unsolvable in that you keep peeling back layers, thinking there's got to be something there," Shea expounded. "But all you get is another layer."

"And another and another," Nora dolefully agreed.

"Such a hard sell," I swigged from my glass. "How can I resist?"

They laughed and Nora excused herself.

"You might want to have an answer by the time I get back from the restroom," she leaned into me. "Ram's got two other offers on the table."

"Sales don't work that way," I called after her. "You can't make up for blowing it the first time."

Shea wondered aloud how committed the place was to a speakeasy conceit, if the restrooms had water closets or an outhouse rather than modern plumbing.

I smiled, but didn't have enough time to build on the joke.

"If I agree to go out with your boring stepson, will you tell me why you gave up live teaching?"

"We haven't had that conversation?"

"Not really. I was waiting for an opportunity to ask when Nora wasn't around to heckle you."

"Ah," Shea ran her thumbs up and down the curve of her wine glass. "You think real answers can't have a sense of humor."

"I'm curious enough to want an answer that's just for me."

That sounded self-absorbed after I said it, so I put myself in a group: "a student."

She looked as though she was going to gently refuse, or say she didn't really know, it was just a feeling, but then launched into an explanation that sounded like something she might say to a class, on video, or in a room full of us.

"Elementary school primes students to see women as teachers of young children, since most children will have nothing but women teachers until middle school. This embeds in them the idea that women are nurturers rather than great thinkers. Later, when they start going to school where it's broken up into periods, and male teachers start to appear, the men often teach the sciences, further reinforcing this notion of men as less emotional, which many people assume is a requirement to be an intellectual."

She took a sip of Syrah as if it were a bottle of water on the lectern before continuing.

"When students reach young adulthood, college age, and they start to develop an identity apart from their family and the friends they grew up with, Mommy and Daddy issues can emerge, with professors unwittingly playing their parts. Daddy professors have it easier. Even if a prof reminds a young man of the father they resent, they don't challenge him. That never went well before, so they figure it won't go well with the surrogate, maybe even worse. And I don't need, nor want, to get into the issues with young women and father figures. But the Mommy professors? Screwed with both genders. The young men lash out, the young women undermine. Not that there's a tremendous number of them. Most students are fine. But it doesn't take many damaged goods to make things uncomfortable."

She stopped, and it was if she turned off the camera, class dismissed. But I was able to stay behind, and drink from the same bottle as her.

I thanked her.

She smiled rather than say you're welcome. Nora would be back at any second, and if she caught the end of our conversation, she would ask what we were talking about, and neither of us had the energy to be in charge of an explanation.

When she returned and sat down, she wasn't interested in anything other than an answer from me.

"So," she said, with enough intensity that she was probably joking.

"So?" I had forgotten what she was referring to.

"About Ram…"

About Ram.

He's good at describing his food. He can identify every flavor in any dish he orders. If there's even a pinch of oregano, or a dash of saffron, he can taste it. These descriptions make up much our conversation when we go out. He's also good at describing the day he has had, or his week. His short-term memory is remarkable. I have no reason to believe he's making any of it up. Nobody would make up such boring details, unless they are supposed to communicate some greater meaning, but he doesn't read anything into them. They are just things that happened, one thing after another.

I cannot recall a specific moment worth sharing about Ram. We have spent a lot of time together, and I find it pleasant, but without lasting images or lines of dialogue. We are a competent production of a romantic comedy. I enjoy going on a date with him, and when it's over, I forget about it until I'm reminded of the name, and when I hear the name, I have agreeable feelings.

What I love is the world our time together creates. It's a place where I finished my degree, where I like my job a lot more than the previous one. I'm a crop insurance adjuster, specializing in citrus. Much like dating Ram, it's not what I had in mind when I surveyed the market, but it utilizes my analytical skills. Catching someone in a lie is easy. Crafting a case that convinces them to stop lying is the hard part.

I try not to hang out with Shea and Nora too often without him, and try not to ask him too often if we're going to hang out with Shea and Nora.

He's about to be the first man to appear in more than one of my family photographs. My older brother seems to like him. He hasn't looked at me to make a face behind his back while they've been talking. Ram is a good audience. My brother can hold court. My sister likes the way he looks. My younger brother waits to make fun of the men I date until after I break up with them, so I may never know how he feels.

When everyone is on their second glass of whatever they're drinking, the call will go out for everyone to take their places so we can squeeze in the photo before dinner. We will strike our pose in the back row. My older brother will make a joke about our second appearance together. Everyone will laugh, even if it's not funny, because they're happy for me and nervous about our future.

They need not be. I'll be thinking about my most recent case, and our next double date with his mother and Shea.

# The Monitor
## (a short story)

Deciding which photographs to post made her feel like the curator of a museum. She figured most of her audience of friends and people labeled as friends had an attention span of about five pictures. Maybe more if she could come up with some witty captions. The key is to tell a story. Perhaps one shot from each act of the day, with the first act being that group photo they took by the entrance, and that picture of the kids asleep in the car as the finale of the five-act structure. Finding equal screen time for each kid throughout the middle acts would be challenging. Each would count how often they appeared. Well, the baby wouldn't count now, but she would someday.

Her baby was sleeping in her crib in the next room, so she had the monitor on. No noise, not a peep, for the last hour. She didn't have to pick up the boys from school for a couple more hours. She was free. Sort of. There was still this work to be done, this collecting and organizing of pictures. Beats doing the laundry, she thought. Oh yeah, she was doing the laundry. But the dryer had another forty minutes before it would signal its conclusion with a polite little ring of a bell, each meek ding spaced about ten seconds apart. Sometimes she missed her old dryer that blasted a relentless buzzing sound until you opened its door. This new insipid little dinger was passive aggressive, like having someone intermittently tap you on the shoulder and remind you to fold the clothes, but if you don't, then hey, that's all right; just a suggestion.

She was sitting at her desk by the window in their bedroom, the baby monitor perched on the windowsill. A sound did come from the monitor, but not a baby sound. It was feedback. She looked out the window and saw the neighbor's garage door opening. When the garage door stopped, so did the feedback. The neighbor backed out of the garage, the door started to close, and the feedback returned, stopping when the garage door stopped closing.

Garage doors, baby monitors, wireless internet connections...she paused a moment to think of the invisible waves flying around her that communicated commands from one thing to another. She wondered how anyone even thought of the concept, and how anyone managed to harness them and make them talk to things for us. She turned her attention back to her computer and continued to click through her photos from the amusement park with the name she couldn't remember, because one company bought it from another and changed the name. She tried to find the appropriate pictures to represent acts two through four. The middle acts are all about conflict. Her audience would appreciate a little honesty about the conflicts between her kids. Just a little honesty, though. A little curated honesty. Not that she had much choice. The only photos that showed them getting along had clearly involved orders to get along.

She also couldn't use any shots with her husband in them. There tended to be a bulge in his eyes and tightness in his smile that made him look more like the children's abductor than their father.

The pictures of her holding the baby looked good. She knew how to play to the camera. Why didn't anyone else?

More static came from the baby monitor. She looked out the window and saw that her neighbor's garage door was still closed. She switched the frequency on the monitor from "A" to "B", and for some reason it worked. All was clear. She managed to find a good picture of the boys waiting in line for a ride. They were laughing in spite of the wait, sharing a sincere moment of joy. Then she remembered: it was because one of them had farted. It worked, though. It was a great shot, perfect for act two, before the peak and the fall.

There were so many options for act three, so many battles to choose from. She was growing frustrated with how honest she may have to be when she heard crying on the monitor. She started to stand up when it dawned on her that the crying was unfamiliar. It was not her baby's cry. It was an adult; a woman's cry. She stared at the monitor, the phantom cry pushing her heart rate faster and higher, up into her neck. She stared at the monitor, then the fuzziness of the neighbor's house through the window behind the monitor took shape.

The garage door.

The feedback earlier.

The neighbor also had a baby, a few months younger than hers. The neighbor's baby was an only child. There had been a few half-hearted attempts to be new mother buddies, some reflexive grins through the car window en route to the garage, a couple of brief hellos and courtesy admirations of each other's babies when stumbling upon each other at the beginning or end of a walk with their strollers, but neither had seemed very interested.

Now she was interested. Assuming it was, in fact, her neighbor crying. She listened closer, trying to hear something else, some other clue. She knew nothing about her neighbor, or the man she lived with. She had never been inside their home. The woman who was crying then started saying something in between sobs.

She eased her computer to the side and leaned over her desk to get closer to the monitor, to the point where she was lying on her stomach across the top of her desk, because she didn't want to move the monitor even slightly and risk losing the signal. Holding perfectly still while spread across her desk with her ear inches away from the speaker and her face narrowed in concentration, she finally started to decipher the words. The crying woman was saying "I can't do it" repeatedly. She would say it several times in a row and then sob some more. "I can't do it." A steady, low hum of static accompanied the episode, rising slightly in intensity and interference each time she said the words.

She heard the woman attempt to gather herself by taking deep breaths intended to overcome the sobs. She started to sniffle more decisively, as though each one was supposed to be the last, her self-imposed signal that it was time to stop crying. Then she heard some noises indicating movement, the static pronouncing each move with a spike in decibel level. A door shut with a crackly burst of radio waves. She figured it was over. She slid back into her chair and continued to stare at the monitor, as though a new voice may come on and explain what just happened.

But it wasn't over. The door opened again with the radio wave accompaniment. There was crying again, only this time it was the baby. The mother had been in the baby's room crying, while the baby was somewhere else in the house, and now the mother was bringing the baby back in the room, and the baby was crying. Intensely. It was one of those sincere cries, not just a signal of hunger or irritation, but a cry that seemed to announce it really hurts to be a baby.

She didn't splay herself across her desk this time; she just kept staring at the monitor as she had been before the baby was brought back into the room. She didn't need to change her position to hear any better. She hadn't moved for several minutes. The baby would seem to be calming down, but then somehow find the energy to bawl even harder than before, the effort needed to keep it up intensifying the effect. She started to wonder about her own baby. She slowly reached out to the monitor, and flipped the frequency back from "B" to "A". Silence. For a moment.

Then she started to pick up the faint sound of crying again, from beyond the monitor. Live, unfiltered crying. She stood up and walked into the hallway and stood at her baby's door, but that wasn't the source. She cracked the door open and peeked inside just to be sure. Still sleeping. She closed the door and walked downstairs, and continued out the front door. She stood in front of her neighbor's house and heard it again. Figuring that the crying being audible from the street gave her an excuse, she walked up to the door and rang the bell. No answer.

She knocked. No answer.

She stood there for a few minutes, and then went back home.

For days afterwards, she would listen to her neighbor on frequency "B". The man she lived with would leave, the garage opening and closing apparently serving as some sort of disruption of the monitor's radio waves, or whatever kind of waves they were. Sometimes she would have to slide the monitor around the windowsill to find the right spot, but eventually she would be able to hear inside the baby's room. The neighbor's baby always had some difficulty getting to sleep for that afternoon nap. Sometimes her own baby would have some difficulty, too, and her eagerness to tune in to the latest episode of her neighbor's struggles made these occasional crises all the more frustrating, as it was hard to hear her neighbor talking to herself with both babies crying, and the talking was the best part.

The days when her neighbor's baby went down relatively easy were particularly interesting, because the neighbor would then talk to her baby. She couldn't make out all the words she was saying, but there were certain expressions that cut through the static, perhaps due to her own familiarity with them, or perhaps because her neighbor felt most comfortable repeating them, and therefore pronounced them with more confidence and clarity: "Things will get better", "There is a reason for everything", "You are the best thing that ever happened to me". But at some point during her monologues, one of these statements would also stop her short and send her out of the room in a hurry, waves of static tracing her pace as she tried to get out of the room before breaking down.

At least that's how she imagined it was playing out. That's how it sounded. She had yet to try and talk to her again since that first day of discovery. She didn't want to knock on the door or ring the bell anymore. At one point she thought maybe her neighbor would be more inclined to answer if she waited a while and gave her a chance to settle down after getting the baby down and talking herself down. But by that time, her own baby would be up, and it would almost be time to pick up the boys from school.

She decided to try and design an encounter with her in the morning during their walks with the strollers, as had happened inadvertently a few times before. It was more difficult than she imagined it would be, however, as the neighbor had developed a routine that involved starting to walk while she was out bringing the boys to school. She suspected this was deliberate, due to her knocking and ringing that first day on frequency B.

So one morning after coming home from dropping off the boys, she left the garage open, put her baby in the stroller, and waited, lurking just out of sight beside the car where she could see through its windows when the neighbor would be coming. Her baby was impatient about being put in the stroller without walking immediately, so she rolled it back and forth as she kept a lookout through the car windows.

Finally the neighbor appeared, headphones on, pushing her stroller. Her chance was finally arriving. But now her baby was the fussy one, being rolled back and forth for several minutes not providing much satisfaction. She had to seize the moment, though, so she did her best to act naturally as she emerged from the garage towards her neighbor's path.

"Hello," she said, pouring on the sunshine before quickly realizing her neighbor was hiding within her headphones and behind her stroller to pretend not to see her. She was about to crash her stroller into her neighbor's, then figured an exaggerated wave would be better.

"Hello," she signaled, arm waving full extension up and down, while her other arm maneuvered her stroller at an angle that would possibly sideswipe the other without hitting it squarely. The neighbor stopped while looking at the ground, as if trying to find some energy for the interaction. She took a deep breath and removed her headphones, which acted as a curtain being raised, her cue to smile as best she could.

"Oh, hello," the neighbor replied, volleying back the manufactured sunshine.

"Been awhile," she said, trying not to tense up over the fact her baby was now in full cry and threatening to scratch the opportunity. "She settles down once we get going," she assured her neighbor, whose baby was asleep.

"Well, don't let us get in your way," said the neighbor, preparing to reaffix her headphones and lower the curtain once more.

"Yours sure has grown," she interjected, "Just adorable."

She rested the headphones back on her shoulders, but kept her hands wrapped around them. "Thank you," she replied dutifully, "Yours too."

They both looked at her now-furious baby.

"Nice of you to say so," she said, trying to make light of the situation. But then she saw her chance. "It is hard sometimes, isn't it?"

The neighbor played a little bit too dumb. "What do you mean?"

"Being a mom," she probed. "It can be really hard."

"I guess," the neighbor shrugged, "Sometimes."

"Look," she decided to go all in. "I hear you having problems over there...sometimes."

The neighbor shot her a sharp look.

She scrambled to think of a way to soften it.

"Just a lot of crying in the afternoon," she qualified her previous statement, not about to give away the situation with the monitor.

"That doesn't mean anything," the neighbor said. "It's just crying. My husband goes to work in the afternoon and works late. She misses her Daddy." Upon mentioning her husband, the neighbor looked nervously over at her house. As though not seeing him in the window or in the doorway put her mind at ease, she then regained her footing on the sunshine. "Babies are a blessing," she smiled.

"Of course they are," she said. And she wanted to say something more, but her baby was unrelenting in her demands, and her neighbor's baby was now starting to stir. Her neighbor pounced on the opening.

"Looks like we'd better get inside for a feeding," she said. "Nice to see you again," she smiled even more broadly, relieved that she was now free to go.

"Nice to see you too."

She watched her neighbor flee towards the front door. She was about to say "if you ever need someone to talk to..." but the headphones were already re-established, and within seconds she was back inside the house. She stood there for a while with her baby's wail echoing through the neighborhood.

The walk settled them both down, mother and child. Upon returning to the house, she spread out a blanket on the floor next to her desk and let her baby roll around and chew on some toys while she moved the monitor from the windowsill to her nightstand. She then completed the visual narrative she had been ignoring. She used more photos than she had initially planned on sharing. Dozens more. She found plenty of individual shots that made for a more pleasant story. Each boy smiled a lot when they were on their own. There was even a usable one of her husband relaxing at a table in front of a concession stand without a trace of tension in his face as the boys were off somewhere. The group photo was still at the beginning, and the picture of the kids sleeping in the car was still at the end. She wrote captions that she hoped would communicate how wonderful it all was, without sounding as though she was trying to rub anyone's face in it.

She toyed with the idea of including a picture of the boys acting up, or her husband tensing up, for comic relief. But she wasn't sure she could make it sound funny enough, and she wouldn't want people to get the wrong idea.

# Marketing
# (a short story)

Perhaps because business is conducted before the sun comes up, when most people are still in bed dreaming, the wholesale flower market seems to float. Two-tiered wagons full of fresh cut blooms drift by, sunflower heads bent over the side, daisy faces pointing straight ahead, lilies lying on their backs. Men in surgeon-like gray pullovers and jumpsuits brush past with armfuls of gladiolas slung over their shoulder, the thick bodies of the gladiolas bouncing in rhythm to the gait of the men in scrubs who shuttle them to vans parked with the back doors open, loud advertisements for the businesses painted across the sides: *Flowers by Junko, Valley Floral, Bridget's Blooms, A Thousand And One Buds.* Hundreds of growers and wholesalers guarding their booths, serving thousands of florists wandering the aisles, at times the pace comparable to that of a stock market exchange floor, but accomplished hours before the alarms of the normal business world sound, before the doors of the 9-to-5 are unlocked. Only when Martin stops and really studies everything, does the market make noise. Once he continues to go about his business, all is silent once more, everything floats. The whole place sleepwalks.

It took Martin a long time to get to know the faces, much less the names. Nobody ever seemed to mind, though. If someone cannot remember a name, there are plenty of jokes to cover for it: *It's early...I haven't had my coffee yet...if we met in the evening, I'd remember you.* But Martin has made his peace with the market, its hours and environment. It is all part of the unspoken deal he has made with his wife. By rising before dawn three days a week, he does not have to cope as much with the consuming public stalking the aisles of the small grocery store he and Veronica own and operate. The wholesale flower market on Wednesdays, the wholesale produce market on Mondays and Fridays, provide Martin with the excuse of being too tired to help out Veronica in the store on those days.

"Oh, Ronnie," he says every time he arrives home at dawn following the market, "do you know how tired I am?" And then Veronica will come up with some absurd guesses they both relish, even if they are not funny to anyone else or have been recycled from some previous morning: "So tired you could eat a horse?" "So tired you're going to dream in near-death experiences?" Martin arrives at the store in time to help close up, however, and he is there every day when he does not have to get up at one in the morning to squeeze peaches or sniff delphinium.

Every so often, Veronica manages to get out of bed and come with him to the flower market, thanks to the little boy. Veronica loves playing with him, cooing in his ear and messing up his hair, playing peek-a-boo. Today is one of those days. Little Anthony is there with his grandmother, who runs one of the stands in the market. The mother is not around. "Still in bed when I left," says the grandmother. "You know how teenagers are."

Martin paces slowly around the stand pretending to look for something. He never buys anything at Amelia's stand. The "fresh" flowers have been refrigerated for some time, their petals littering the floor around the buckets, and the dried flowers are covered with dust. But he has to do something to bide his time at the moment. Veronica and Amelia are discussing the hardships in raising a child. Martin and Veronica have raised two, both now grown and on their own. Martin wonders why their conversation is even taking place. It is not Amelia's child, not the grandmother's responsibility. It is her daughter's. Martin has a hard time referring to Amelia as a *grandmother*. She is a more appropriate age to have a one-year-old son than her daughter is, which means, of course, that Amelia had her daughter at a young age as well.

"Does your family still grow, Amelia?" Martin asks, as he picks up a bouquet of carnations from a bucket and lets the stems shed loud drops of water into the bucket.

Amelia stops talking to Veronica. "No," she says, "we haven't grown for some time. We're just wholesalers now. We mostly buy imports."

"I thought so," says Martin, letting the carnations fall back into the bucket.

Veronica stops playing with Anthony and glares at Martin, who catches her look and tries to explain himself. "It's just a bit cold for carnations around these parts."

"We used to own some greenhouses," says Amelia, her posture rising with pride for a moment.

"Oh, really?" says Martin.

"Yes," answers Amelia, "my grandfather used to raise a lot of carnations."

"Your grandfather, really?" adds Veronica, acting overly-fascinated.

"Oh, yes," Amelia savors the attention, "he was one of the best growers in the market."

"Well," says Martin, easing his way towards the exit, "I guess you know what to buy, then."

"Oh, sure," Amelia smiles, "I know my stuff." Her teeth are gray from smoking.

Before joining Martin outside the stand, Veronica buys a dried flower arrangement which has been sitting on Amelia's old metal desk for months. Martin points this out to Amelia as they walk away together.

"I don't care," snaps Veronica. "I only bought it to try and make up for you acting like such a prick."

"I'm sorry," says Martin. "I just get annoyed when you start drooling over that kid."

"What are you, jealous? He's just a little boy."

"He's doomed," Martin says. "Look at him. It's...what?" he looks at his watch. "It's three-thirty in the morning, the kid's running around like it's recess. What else is he going to do with his life getting used to these hours? How is he going to stay awake in school?"

"What's wrong with following in the family business?"

"There is no family business, Veronica. They sold it years ago. Amelia works for somebody else, by the hour, no benefits. And Anthony's gonna end up pushing carts around the market for a few bucks with the rest of the guys they pluck off the street."

"How do you know they sold the business?"

"It's common knowledge around here."

"Well...is that any excuse to be mean to a little boy?"

Martin sighs. "I'm not being mean. I just wish people would stop being all cuddly with that gang and tell them how they're ruining that kid. He's not going to be cute forever."

Veronica becomes quiet, and they do not speak much to each other the rest of the morning. Strictly business: what product they can move, what looks fresh, what colors appeal to their clientele. As they head back to the car with their last purchase, Veronica says she's going to say good-bye to Anthony. She takes a long time. Martin falls asleep in the car. The door slams, waking him. Veronica has a big smile on her face.

"He kissed me," she says. "It was the cutest thing."

***

Martin is the only one in the store late Saturday night when it is robbed.

"Under the drawer," says the kid wearing a ski mask, the pistol in his hand quivering "Anything under the drawer?"

"Under the drawer?" Martin asks.

"Under that thing, that thing that separates the bills and shit. The plastic thing."

"Oh, under that thing, yeah." Martin lifts it up and shows the kid a couple of fifty dollar bills underneath. Martin has been robbed several times before; definitely more times than this kid has attempted robberies.

"Well?" says the kid.

"What?"

"Give it to me. Gimme those fifties."

"Oh, yeah. Sure." Martin lays the fifties on the counter, and the kid stuffs them into his pockets. "Tell me something," Martin asks him. "How old is your mother?"

The eyes inside the ski mask narrow. The mouth falls open. Martin continues.

"You're about what, nineteen? Twenty?"

"Shut up," says the kid.

"I'm not playing any trick on you. I just want to know. How old's your mother? Mid-thirties, I'll bet."

"She's about thirty-five, I think," stammers the kid. "You got a safe in back?"

"Could you say that a little louder?" Martin asks, cupping his ear.

"You got a safe in back!"

"No, the part about your mother. How old is she?"

"She's thirty-five, I think."

"Louder. So the surveillance camera can pick it up." Martin points up above to the camera. "We've got audio."

The kid says it nice and loud, as though in a school play. He even looks at the camera.

***

Veronica and Martin hover over their kitchen table at home watching the video of the robbery on their computer.

"For God's sake, Martin. You could have been killed."

"Nonsense. Look at him. Wouldn't kick a dog. Just listen, listen to how old his mother is."

"I heard him the first time. Is that a real gun?"

"And how old do you think Amelia's daughter is? Fifteen, maybe?"

Veronica turns away from the screen and towards her husband. "You mean to tell me," she says, very slowly, "that you risked your life to win an argument?"

"We weren't arguing," says Martin, "listen to this…" He gestures back to the screen. The kid mentions that his mother always passed him off to his grandmother. "See?" Martin wags his finger towards the screen. "See what I mean? Anthony doesn't have a chance."

"It's just one robber, Martin, one kid. Have you reported this to the police?"

"You know what good that does."

"So you haven't."

"No."

Veronica looks up at the ceiling and sighs. "We spend thousands on a surveillance system, and you use it to try and win an argument."

"We weren't arguing."

A loud blast from the video startles Veronica. She stares at the screen. The blast was so loud that the only noise now accompanying the picture is static gurgling from the speakers as the surveillance microphone tries to recover from the jolt to its system. The kid is stuffing the gun down his pants as he runs out of the store, and Martin crumples to the floor behind the cash register. Veronica looks from the image of Martin on the screen, to his presence next to her as he stands up straight and folds his arms.

"He hit the coffee pot," he explains. "He wanted to scare me, so he used the gun. He was definitely aiming for the coffee machine, not me. He really was."

The static fades from the speakers, and Martin's moans and curses are heard now on the video. Veronica turns and watches him writhe in pain, and struggle to get on his feet.

He leans over and speaks softly into her ear. "Some shards of glass cut my arm. I made it over to aisle seven: first aid supplies."

He unbuttons his shirt and pulls down the sleeve to reveal a bandage wrapped around his bicep. She stares at the wrapping as Martin reaches around her and minimizes the video. They stare at each other. She continues removing his shirt for him. They kiss and he leans her back onto the kitchen table, which is only the first place they end up making love that night. They wake up several hours later on the living room floor, laughing at themselves.

***

They try to pass by Amelia's stand without her seeing them, but she does. She waves frantically and rushes towards them.

"Long time, no see," she says to Veronica.

"I haven't been able to wake up early enough," she tells Amelia. "That's Martin's job."

"Anthony will be so happy to see you," says Amelia.

Martin and his wife look at each other. "No," says Veronica, "that's okay, don't wake him."

"Oh, Veronica, you know he's always up. Anthony!"

Anthony comes stumbling out from the back, a sprig of dried baby's breath in his fist. He sees Veronica, and his face splits into a huge grin. He runs towards her, but she does not bend down on one knee to greet him. She remains upright, and gives Anthony a pat on the head as he clutches her leg.

"Hello there, Anthony," she says. "We're pretty busy today, Amelia. Could I just get a couple of those wreaths off the wall? We did really well with those last Christmas."

Amelia hesitates, catches herself staring at Veronica, then does what she is told. Anthony releases himself from Veronica's leg. He looks up at her, but she continues to watch Amelia reach for the wreaths on the wall, which are just beyond her grasp. Anthony looks over at Martin, who smiles at him. The boy's eyes begin to collapse, and Martin turns away before the crying comes.

# Over Here We Have
# (a novelette)

*Dr. Diego Alejo*

"Sixty-seven million dollars."

I heard him try to clear his throat, but he couldn't quite follow through.

"I'm sorry?" he needed to hear it again.

"Sixty-seven. We need these kids to generate sixty-seven million dollars."

"That's three times what you normally need."

"It is."

"That's pretty much your operating budget for the year."

"It is."

"Okay...um..." I heard his chair squeak and a pencil or pen tap on his desk. The sound quality of his speaker phone was top notch.

"Yes," I said.

"What?"

"The answer to the question you're trying to ask. Yes. We are in massive financial trouble."

"I gathered. But why?"

"Come on. Seriously?"

"Okay, but Diego, to that degree? Good Lord. Forty-five million more than average? I thought your enrollment only went down, like, two or three percent."

"For the fall semester," I stood up and looked out my office window. "Once they got a load of our online courses, they bailed. We were down fifteen percent by winter break."

"Don't you have some kids living on campus?"

"We do," I watched a lone student stare at her phone while sitting on the edge of a fountain that had not been turned on since the day we were ordered to retreat last spring. "But not enough of them to cover the cost of our food service and maintenance contracts. We're a small school, Raj. And we're drowning."

"And you're going to grab on to as many rich families as you can."

"We're going to try," I verified his conclusion.

Raj took a long drag on a sigh.

"I can't imagine this was your idea."

"No," I joined him in a sigh. "It's against everything they hired me to do. But these are desperate times."

"So they fall back on past measures."

"It's both extremely radical and not at all innovative."

"Kind of impressive in its own right."

"That's why I didn't put up much of a fight. I couldn't help but admire the hutzpah. Plus I'm outranked by about twenty people who all signed on."

"I take it they've assured you this is only temporary."

"A one-year stopgap," I imitated the announcement. "And it's going to be the easiest application season of my career."

"Easiest of mine, too. At least with your school."

"I'll have plenty of time to put out some applications of my own."

"I hope you land at another college we work with."

"Am I your favorite client?"

"Absolutely."

"And you don't say that to all your other clients?"

"Not all of them."

I turned away from the window as the student walked away from the dry fountain.

"At the risk of sounding shifty," I sank back into my chair. "Dr. Emory Withers and his board of minions, er, trustees, respectfully ask that you keep this on the down-low."

"I can see why."

I reclined far enough to stare at the ceiling, which inspired some meditation on our situation.

"You'd think having to keep this quiet would convince them maybe it's not the best way to mount a comeback."

"It's not illegal," Raj tried to sound reassuring. "You're a private institution."

"We'll be doling out a few scholarships," I flipped my chair back to an upright position. "Full rides only. We're cobbling together our hodgepodge of partials into some splashy offers."

"Human shields."

"Pretty much."

"Have you cleared it with the donors?"

"They're all dead."

"No wonder you're under water. Who's in charge of your endowment?"

"I'm kidding. They're not all dead. Only most of them. The donor names are still on each award, we're just funneling multiple scholarships to the lucky few. Meanwhile we're offering every accepted student a seven thousand dollar president's grant, which is really a ten percent tuition discount across the board, but that sounds desperate, so we're calling it a president's grant."

"A president's grant," he mused. "And Emory didn't name it after himself?"

"The Withers Award," I proclaimed.

We both reveled in the sound of it.

"Not under these circumstances," I continued. "Aside from not having much of a ring to it, if this blows up, he needs all the escape routes he can manage. Oh, and if a student has been recruited by one of our coaches into the high-stakes world of Division Three intercollegiate sports, we're tacking on three grand and calling it an athletic scholarship."

"You've got a legacy to keep up. I don't think I've seen a campus with so many banners dedicated to D3 sports."

"You need to come out and visit us again if that's your most vivid memory."

"We can catch a water polo match."

I released a melancholy laugh.

"I've never been to a game before," I realized. "Water polo, football, softball, none of the above. Now I can't wait to go to one. Next year. If we're still here."

"I like your chances," he sounded more encouraging than convinced. "You've got nice weather and a short drive to civilization. If you were the same size with the same price tag but out in the sticks, someplace where the sun doesn't shine from November to May, I'd say sayonara."

I ended our conversation on that positive note. I thanked him for the words of encouragement and said we would get back to him shortly with our first round of candidates, which for the first time in a decade of working together, would probably be our only round.

I grabbed my coat for the walk to our admissions bunker, which is what we named a conference room in the Career Center that we took over every year after winter break to scan applications and bargain with each other over prospective students as if they were Pokémon cards.

I made my way through the empty corridors of the administration building. Everyone else was working from home. As with any walk across our campus, my walk to the Career Center was a short one. The day was sunny with a windless bite in the air, my favorite weather combination. I could make the trip with my eyes closed, especially with nobody around, and did so for several paces to focus on how the temperature cooled my face while the sun warmed it.

I heard a young woman's voice echo across the premises, and opened my eyes to see a tour group appear from around the corner of the Career Center, heading for the quad. A half-dozen pods of families kept their distance from each other and wore masks, part of our effort to generate enthusiasm for the following year, when we assumed enough doses of vaccine would reach enough people to make enough prospective students feel comfortable enough to come back and allow us to play to our strengths as a cozy, monitored, manicured station on the trip to adulthood. The tour guide was doing her best to crank that image in spite of making their way through so few signs of life. There were no people, only places.

It only took me about thirty seconds to reach the Center after I spotted them, but in that span she used the phrase "over here we have" four times. Over here we have Ostrander Park, named after the family that donated the land that our college is located on, and over here we have the largest juice bar on campus, which is also the largest juice bar in the county. There were a couple of other things we had over here, but I tuned them out and concentrated on the phrase, not only how often she said it, but how its meaning could change with a shift in inflection. I said it to myself, and emphasized the word "we", so rather than refer to location, it referred to ownership. Look at all that we have. Over here, here, here, and here. It's all ours.

I felt like a tour guide of sorts when I entered the admissions bunker, ready to lead those in my charge toward our goal. Most years, our vision of the incoming class took shape as we sifted through the applicants, but some years had a mandate.

"This is one of those years," I announced as I took my place at the table.

Our table was actually several narrow tables lined up in a square. All six of us were present. I sat alone on one side, the Associate Dean of Admissions sat across from me on the other, and there were two admissions officers on each of the other sides. No masks were necessary. One of our trustees was also on the board of a local hospital. He had lobbied to get us vaccinated earlier than our health profiles would have otherwise allowed. His rationale was that the college is a vital economic engine for the community, and our admissions team needed to meet as soon as possible and extend invitations to students to save us from insolvency. The irony was that this year required no finesse, just a cash grab, and we could have easily done it through a video conference. I could have done it myself, but I played along to keep my team employed.

I had already emailed them all and spoken with each of them over the phone, but I felt a need to set the tone.

"We've got a mandate," I reminded them. "An extremely specific one."

I looked around the table and waited until everyone looked up from their laptops before proceeding.

"Some of you were here back when the college had their credit rating lowered, so we couldn't be as generous in finding ways to offer money to students we really fell in love with."

Scanning their faces, I realized none of them were there during that infamous year of the credit drop. They had all been hired during our heady days of overspending. The point stood, though, so I pushed on.

"Since then it's been a love fest, bending over backwards to get the class we want, running a revised list by Raj at the analytics firm every couple of days, trying to find the perfect balance between high-need students and low-need until we hit our number. And someday we'll be able to do that again. But not this year. This year is no-need. This year we do our best impression of a college from those bygone days when people simply sent their kid and paid the bill."

"At least hitting the number will be easy," said Associate Dean Edna from across the square and over her reading glasses. "Which is ironic given what a huge number it is."

"The capture rate is the key," said our youngest, a kid named Jeff who looked like he should be submitting an application rather than evaluating them. "We need more students than usual to commit to us for that number to save us."

"With that," I bounced off his point and stood up to set our agenda.

The tray along the bottom of the white board only had three markers. The first two were dry.

"Drumroll please," I teased as I reached for the third.

It worked, squeaking as I used it to draw two dots, one on top of the other, accompanied by exaggerated applause from the team.

Next to the top dot, I wrote *No FAFSA*.

Next to the second dot, I wrote *No business being here.*

The applause morphed into anxious laughter as I turned to face them, marker still in hand.

"These are the two prime directives for this first round of screening," I announced. "If the applicant's family has not submitted a Financial Aid form, that of course means money is no object. And if the applicant's academic record makes you wonder why they bothered to apply, if their extracurricular activities are blatantly padded and their personal essay barely literate, even better. We're starting at the bottom, folks. Disregard the rock stars, we'll get to them later. For now, we're looking for that sweet intersection of wealth and mediocrity. We want families who are going to be grateful to us for taking their little slackers off their hands."

I dropped the marker in the tray and tried to read the room, but all I decoded was shock. My emails and phone calls had been less emphatic.

Imelda, our mercenary, raised her hand. We were her fifth college in her ten years as an officer. I was surprised she raised her hand before speaking. I guessed she wanted to be called on for dramatic effect. I obliged, and my guess was correct. She lowered her hand more slowly than necessary.

"This goes against everything I got into admissions for," she said, pausing long enough for the others to consider whether they should say something similar. "And I can't wait to do it."

The nerves from all previous laughter were expelled. We erupted into a spasm of elation, a loud admission of guilt and deviant pleasure.

"Thank God no one else is in the building," Edna wheezed as she removed her glasses and wiped her eyes.

We settled in to our work, but every five minutes someone, usually Imelda or Jeff, would share a canned line from a personal essay ("My lacrosse brothers and me are like soldiers storming the battlefield"), the guarded words of a forced letter of recommendation ("Britt participated in every group project required of her"), or an innocuous activity contorted into something meant to sound impressive ("Assisted in editing social media announcements for Advanced Choir"), and we would crack up all over again.

Reyna resisted reading aloud. She was the chosen one in the eyes of our president and his college cabinet. Reyna would jump Edna and be offered my position if I ever left. But she laughed as loud as the rest of us, and in place of sharing what was on her screen, she would narrate her feelings about what she read.

"It's horrifying and liberating all at once," she said as lunch drew near.

Len, our Regional Advisor, spoke up.

"I know," he said. "It reminds me of the first time I did crank."

Those were his first words of the day.

He was my first hire after they brought me on as Director of Admissions. I didn't want someone too chatty, since students find that phony, but I went too far in the other direction. I was convinced Len had a wise quality. Maybe he did back then, but the job involved long stretches of sitting behind tables of brochures at college fairs, or sitting in high school counseling centers during lunch trying to lure students with free pizza, and the perpetual stupor it put him in eventually engulfed any flair I imagined was there. I'm sure I wasn't the only one who thought Len on crank might be an improvement.

Our fingers froze on our keyboards. Everyone looked at each other, then at Len, who continued to scroll through his screen for a few seconds before realizing we were all staring at him.

"First and last time," he clarified.

Our laughter was a slower build that never reached the same volume as our previous bouts, but lasted longer, a sustained snicker we failed to resist all the way to lunch.

"If that's the only thing he says all day, Len will be my favorite colleague of all time," Reyna said later as she and I dined while sitting on a bench that lined the quad. "And I have about twenty-five years left in this business."

"It will be the only thing he says all day," I predicted, then raised my water bottle in a toast. "Here's to your favorite colleague of all time."

She was the only member of our team who shared my affection for crisp sunny days. She met my bottle with hers, and expressed appreciation for the sandwich she ordered with a long hum during her latest bite.

"I'm so glad we didn't eat at the dining hall," she added.

"They're working on a thin margin," I reminded her of our rationale for ordering out from everyone's favorite nearby deli. "We wouldn't want to take food from the mouths of our students."

"Be sure to write that on the reimbursement form."

"I'm going to save it in case I'm called in front of the VP."

She nodded her approval as she took a swig of water.

"Do you think it's because we're from the East Coast that we like this kind of weather?" she asked upon completing her gulp.

"Could be."

"I mean, this kind of day, this time of year? My friends and I would be out in shorts and tanks tops."

"We're an adaptable species."

"We are," she agreed, nodding long enough to signal she was thinking of redirecting the conversation. I gave her the space to do so.

"Do you think you'll be able to live with yourself when these acceptance letters go out?" she asked.

"So," I crumpled up the paper that had been wrapped around my wrap. "The conversation turns toward the elephant."

"I know, sorry. But now that we're taking a break, I'm starting to think more about this."

"I've been thinking about it ever since the order came down."

"Good," she put aside her sandwich, fully invested in our talk. "Not that I'm surprised. They brought you out here for a reason, and you've been fulfilling it beautifully. This school is miles ahead of where it was before you arrived."

"Thank you."

"And we're backed into a corner, I get it. First things first. You can't diversify a school that doesn't exist."

"But?"

"Isn't this a bit much?" she looked bewildered.

I took a sip of my own and considered how to put her more at ease.

"The best and brightest we invite to come here never do," I said. "Not to denigrate our students. They're great. What we tell them is true, there are no safety schools nowadays. Getting in almost anywhere is an accomplishment. But you know what I'm talking about. I've seen your disappointment when we don't hear back from the names you fought for."

"How is lowering our standards going to help that?"

"I'm not talking about us. This is about the students. They'll be fine. Those wonderful people you're concerned about, they're going to land on their feet, at the schools they would have chosen anyway. And you won't have to worry about being rejected by your crushes, because we won't invite them in the first place."

"No one to fight for," she lamented, ignoring my punch line.

"You've got the bonus babies," I reminded her. "We'll offer those kids the world, and with so few of them, you can recruit them like you're some millionaire football coach at a national powerhouse."

"I'm not sure I have it in me to be that obnoxious."

My analogies and punch lines flailing, I reverted back to mentor mode.

"If you decide this is more of a compromise than you can live with, you can always move on. I'm sure you could land a job with pretty much any school on the U.S. News Top 100."

"What about you?" she seemed slightly more at peace.

A reflexive chuckle prevented me from taking my last sip of water.

"When I was on the phone with Raj, I mentioned I would have plenty of time to fill out applications of my own since this season is going to be so easy. I was half-joking, but I think I will check to see what's out there."

"Then I guess I'll have to go with my second choice," she said. "You'll get any job ahead of me."

"Only if we have to shut down," I said. "If this works, you better believe I'm sticking around next year to see what happens."

We both laughed and realized we sounded like a couple of villains, so we played it up and started rubbing our hands together and twirling our invisible mustaches.

*Dr. Sophia Ulrich*

Something was wrong.

I've been doing this long enough to roll with a certain amount of student apathy, particularly toward the end of the semester, but this was an aggressive form of apathy, from day one, concentrated in the first-year students, who wordlessly dared you to do something about it.

All the other students seemed happy to be back. The upper division students, as a whole, were the best I had in years, perhaps my career. The second-years were just as enthusiastic, if a little rusty, since it was their first year of college in person. But those first years? They never even looked at me. They looked at the floor, the tabletop, the ceiling, sometimes straight ahead at nothing in particular. They tried to look at their phones, but our small classrooms make that impossible. Discussions were a brush with insanity. I could see people around me, and tried to talk to them, but they ignored me, going about their business of not caring, as though I was playing a ghost in a stage production. Their work was worse than bad. It made no impression. I started to wish it was bad, rather than opening up a void like it did. Their essays read like something written by a committee. I'm certain they were plagiarizing, but I could never find the source. They were probably using an essay app on the dark web that came free with their drug order.

My colleagues also had a hard time catching their eye and catching them cheating.

I arranged meetings with as many of my fellow professors as our schedules allowed, to compare notes and try to invent a cure, if we made it that far. We usually couldn't stop bitching long enough to brainstorm solutions. I even met with colleagues I didn't care for, like Abel Munari, so I could widen my sample and make sure that support for my observations wasn't a result of shared sensibilities among my preferred group.

Abel had never done anything to me personally, like Eve Wilmer did when she was the curriculum rep for our department. She helped me develop a new course on the influence of wet nurses in the curation of Medieval aristocratic values, and then cast the deciding vote that prevented it from being adopted. I vowed never to speak to her again. A year later she left for a job at some mini-Ivy in Maine, so it's been an easy vow to keep.

No, Abel Munari was one of those "kids these days" old guys who accuse younger generations of being soft, even though he came of age when it was possible to work a minimum wage job to pay your way through college, and he probably had twelve offers to teach when he finished his PhD. He carried himself as if he had fought the Nazis, but was born a generation later, and didn't even fight the War on Drugs. I struck up conversations with him when I wanted to gain a perspective from the other side.

We met at a popular off-campus deli that had weathered the shutdown thanks to being the primary take-out option for those hearty few who worked and lived on campus during the economic storm. Abel thought using a lot of swear words helped him connect with students, and his voice had been growing louder every year after he hit age sixty, so I made sure to meet him in the late afternoon, after the lunch rush, so hardly anybody would have to overhear him.

"Bar none, the worst fucking batch of students I've ever been stuck with," he declared.

I figured as much.

He expounded.

"They're not naturally stupid. They're far worse. They're lazy. They've made a conscious choice to be ignorant. They're an entire incoming class of the kind of student I fucking hate."

I looked around to see if anyone was listening. The only other person seated at a table looked like a student, but she had earbuds in. The staff was busy behind the counter cleaning up after the rush, excited the worst was over, talking to each other loudly.

"Case in point," he slid his coffee to the side, clearing space for his hand gestures. We had both already eaten before our meeting, which was a relief to the staff when we showed up while they were preparing to close and we just ordered a coffee and a bottle of juice. "The other day in my Civics intro class, we're discussing the Voting Rights Act being rolled back in certain states, and I rush through a quick review of it being passed into law. I drop the name Lyndon Johnson. Some kid says 'Who?'"

"Uh oh."

"I didn't lose my shit," he assured me. "I learned very early this semester that this is a very different group of kids, and I need to give them a long leash or else I'm gonna start screaming in class someday and never stop. So I patiently explained he was the president at the time, and some other moron says 'There was a president named Lyndon? I thought we never had a woman president.' Which causes some giggling. I actually found that encouraging. Wow, a pulse, you know? So I try to ride the merriment to some peace of mind. I say, 'Not to single anyone out, but just to make sure, everyone else knows who Lyndon Johnson is, right?' Nope. No one. Not one hand goes up, no heads nod. I try one more time, ask them if seriously, no one knows who the fuck Lyndon Johnson is. Nothing."

"Oh my," I was right there with him.

"I don't know where to go from there. I can't continue the conversation. I'm floored. I put my hands on my knees and tried to think of what to do next. I almost told them to get the fuck out and watch the History Channel or something, but then I got real curious. I stood up and asked them to write down the names of five presidents they know other than Trump, Obama, Lincoln, and Washington. I didn't want to embarrass anyone, so I said when they had their list ready, to call me over and I'd check it out."

He paused and stared into space, but not for dramatic effect. His trauma was genuine.

"Not one of them made it to five. There was some George Bush here and there, but nobody realized they could use that name twice. Several Clintons, some Reagans and Kennedys, a few Jeffersons. A Roosevelt, misspelled and no first name. There was a Nixon in there. And get this...John Tyler."

"Who?"

"Exactly," he slapped the table. "You don't even know who that is, and you're a college professor. He was the tenth president. I think. I'm not sure, because there was a president named Taylor soon after, and

I get them confused. How the fuck did this kid know him? He's one of the most forgettable presidents with the most forgettable name. I could see knowing Martin Van Buren, or Millard Fillmore. Those are fun names. But John Tyler? I think I've had a few kids in my classes over the years named John Tyler, but I'm not sure, because why would I remember that name? I asked the kid if he was a member of the Tyler family, if John Tyler was his great-great-great-great grandfather or some shit. Nope. He didn't know how he knew, he just knew. And I can't think of a more useless thing to know about U.S. History. There are things just as useless, but nothing more useless. How does a person know John Fucking Tyler and not know Lyndon Fucking Johnson? This kid has got to be the only person in the whole world where those two things intersect. The only one. Nobody else could possibly know that one thing and not know the other thing. Nobody."

He reached for his coffee.

"Points for originality," he raised his cup before taking a sip and settling down.

I heard similar tales of woe from other instructors, but with less detail and fewer f-bombs.

The kitchen staff told me stories, too, as they scooped up my order of mac and cheese and looked around to make sure no students were in earshot before handing me my plate and reporting that the youngest kids on campus were the ones most often hung over and shuffling through the dining hall in bathrobes and slippers.

Campus police had never broken up so many parties in the first-year dorms, more in the first month than they normally do all year. By the second month they had stopped, because a gang of first-years rented two houses off campus that were strictly for parties, which were patrolled by the city police.

The classified staff didn't have any stories about the incoming class, because they had little to no interaction with them. Hardly any first-year students would show up for advising sessions, or go to the library, or use the tutoring services in the Success Center. Though the ones who did were delightful.

"I hope the rest are so smart they don't need our services," said the director of our Success Center.

"The problem with small sample sizes," I dashed her hope.

I wanted to hear the perspective of the first-years themselves, but didn't think any of them would reveal much, if I could even get one to sit down with me. I got as close as I could by speaking with a student I was advising for her senior project during a scheduled conference in my office.

Delilah was one of the editors of our campus news. When I asked her if she or any of her friends noticed anything off about the incoming class, she and they were way ahead of the rest of us.

"We're doing a story on the first-year problem," she announced. "We've already got a title: *Incoming!* You know, like a bomb flying at you."

"So it's that pronounced."

"Oh, totally," she rolled her eyes. "They make me ashamed I ever laughed at those movies about college where the dipshits are the heroes."

"I'd like to talk to some of them," I confided. "But they're impossible to catch. They sprint for the door as soon I dismiss class, none of them come to office hours, and they can't be threatened with a zero or lured by extra credit."

"We have a first-year on staff who's interviewing as many as she can."

"There's a first-year on your staff?"

"She's one of the good ones."

"I've heard rumors of their existence."

"Got a full ride academic scholarship. She's fantastic, actually. And we're like you, we figured they wouldn't talk to any of us."

"How's she doing with the interviews?"

"All right, but it's taking a while. They love talking about how much fun they're having, but she has a hard time getting them to talk about their applications and how they got here, what high school was like. We don't think they're here by accident. It's not some amazing coincidence that, like, ninety-five percent of the freshman class are morons. Plus our acceptance rate actually went down this year. We became harder to get into, and stupider at the same time. We want to interview people from the Admissions Office."

"Any luck?"

"Eh..." she hedged. "We're kind of scared to ask."

"Why? They don't have any control over you. Not once you got in."

"Yeah, but they're like, connected to the whole machine, you know?"

I decided on the topic of my next paper. It had been a while since I was published.

"Tell you what," I led into a showy pause. "I'll help. I know a couple of them pretty well."

"Thank you," she said, her relief audible.

"One of the benefits of teaching at a small school. If we were at some big state university, I probably wouldn't even know the names of anyone in admissions."

"That's why I came here," she smiled. "The sense of community."

I smiled back and wondered if our minds were as much of a match as our mouths, if she was also hoping that we could do more than merely expose what happened, and return our community to what it was before the intrusion. It would have felt like being a couple of territorial housewives in a 1950s suburb, but in our case the gatecrashers were whiter and wealthier than we were.

*Troy*

I'm gonna try not to use any slang, because I want this to last. I have this one professor, for my Civics class, I can't remember what it's called, Intro to Civics maybe, I'd have to look it up, and he tries too hard to be cool. He cusses all the time. I guess that's what the cool kids did when he was younger, or the cool teachers, who knows, and I don't want this to be cool, I just want people to know forever how much I love it here. I mean really, really, really love it here for real. This place is awesome.

This girl from the school newspaper interviewed me, and got me thinking. It's really a website. There's no paper. I've never read a newspaper. I've seen them in old movies, so I know what they are. People still use that word for some reason. Newspaper. I don't like writing. I hate the feeling of a pen in my hand. It hurts. I get a cramp. That's why I'm doing a video.

I'm not sure what this is going to be. I'm just putting myself out there. Keeping it real. I didn't have enough time to tell that girl what I wanted to say. She kinda surprised me, just came up and started talking to me. "Tell me about your time here so far, what do you like to do, do you like it here?" All that kinda stuff. I've had some time to think about it since then. This is like a love letter, or what we send now days instead of a love letter, because you can see the person and that's better. It's from the heart, for real, no scratching things out and rewriting stuff. That's cheating.

I don't know what's gonna happen to this, and I don't care. If nobody ever sees it and it gets like seventeen views, that's cool. If it goes viral or something, that's cool too. I didn't make it into the article in the school paper. But that's fine, because I didn't want my words all twisted around. That's what the media does. I wanna figure out why I love this place, in real time, for real. I know in my gut I love it, but I wanna start thinking of the reasons. That's why I thought a list would be good. I did this when I liked two girls in eighth grade. I made a list of what I liked about each one to see which list had more things on it, then I chose that girl.

I admit I wanted to go to USC. My name says it. I was born to go there. But I didn't grow big enough. I'm not the most talented player, either, but I work harder than anyone else. You may beat me, but you're not gonna outwork me. Go ahead and take a break. I'm still out there, training, working out, practicing. I'll catch you later. That's one of the reasons I love it here. It may be D3 ball, but they take it seriously, like me. I can ball out here for two years, show the world my toughness and my heart, transfer to a D1 program, then go pro. Maybe not in the NBA, but overseas. Like one of those Euro leagues, or Australia. Go ahead and doubt me. People who doubt me end up regretting it. They look stupid.

I wish more people came to our games. That's one thing I don't like. The gym's pretty much empty when we play. It sucks. If we drew like football, they'd cut us just as much slack as they cut the football team. Instead, they try to make up for it with us. They take out all their punishment on us. Like there was this big-ass koi that swam around the pond in the Founders Garden on campus, and everyone loved that fish. It would come up and dominate all the other koi and get all the attention and food, so some of the first-year football players caught it and put it in a bucket and brought it to Party House Two one night. They thought it would be fun to have it right there at the party and everyone could feed it and pet it and have it suck their fingers and stuff, but the bucket was too small or something and it ran out of air, or whatever fish breathe, and it died. They only got suspended one game. They killed everyone's favorite koi, and all they got was a one-game suspension. Meanwhile two of my buddies and me like to get high in a sand trap next to the thirteenth green on the golf course behind Party House One, and one night Mason took a dump in the hole. Not cool, I know. But it was pretty funny, just one of those stupid things you do when you're young. We didn't kill anything, and we got three games each. All of us. Jett and me wouldn't snitch on Mason, so we all went down together. We had each other's backs. The president, I think his name is Dr. Weathers, said they would have made us clean it up, but the golf course couldn't afford to wait and find out who did it, so they had to scoop it out and open up for the day. Mason said the president could shit in the hole and we could clean up that load if he really wanted us to have the experience. He didn't say it to his face. He said it to us later on at a party after like five beers. Three fucking games. That just made me work harder. I shot like five hundred free throws and a thousand three-pointers that night before the party, and partied harder than ever before. That's just me, man. Everything I do, I go hard.

I love the free parking, too, right by the dorms. You get a sticker from your RA, and boom. I don't drive much, but I like having my car around because sometimes we need to change things up, so we'll drive down to where all the restaurants are by the freeway and pound some Taco Bell or Chick Fil-A, or drive to some of the other colleges and look for parties in those neighborhoods. We ended up at a high school party once. We didn't know for a while, and probably shoulda left when we found out, but we were like Gods, for real. It felt awesome. So we just rolled with it, and that ended up being maybe the most lit night of the year. Top three, for sure. I don't know what the other two would be, since pretty much every night here is lit. That's why we never cruised by that high school house again. It was fun and all, but no need. It was probably just on because someone's parents were out of town, anyway. Around here we're on every night, all night.

I love the girls here. Like ninety percent of them aren't stuck up at all. In our class. All the older ones walk around like they're adults and shit, like they work for the government or some big business, like they make the world go around. Yeah, okay. Whatever you say, girls. I shouldn't say that, come to think of it. The guys are just as bad. There's even some on our team who act like they're all above everyone. This one dude even quit the team senior year so he could do some kind of internship with some company. Seriously? You're gonna quit on us senior year? He wasn't the best player or anything, but dude. What kind of teammate are you? You made a commitment. Honor that. If you can't put in the work for your team, how are you gonna put in the work anywhere else? I didn't even quit on my ultimate Frisbee team, and that's just a club sport. When I signed up, I rode it all the way to the end. We were in the semifinals and our match started a half hour after one of my midterms started, so I finished that test before everyone else in the class and was out the door and on the field before the first pull.

And yeah, it's cool I can get a degree here. Dad says I only have to get a Bachelor's to help him run the business. He used to say I needed to get a MBA, but lowered the deal when he saw how much I love basketball. I'm so glad he did that. Not just so I can focus on my game, but we have people getting Master's degrees here, and you never even see them around. All they do is come to class. I saw these, like, adults going into a classroom one day, and I'm all, "Who are you?" I thought it was a sales meeting for some company that rented the room, or some motivational speaker was going on, but some woman who looked like she had kids told me what was up, that it was a class. I called my Dad right after that lady and me talked and I'm all, "Thank you, Dad. Oh my God, thank you." I told him it's gonna pay off. I'm in the gym every day, getting after it. This senior on our team told me to chill out once. I was up in my buddy's face for not working hard enough. He said he was gonna skip his last set of squats, and no way I was gonna let that happen. So this punk senior says, "It's D3, man. Relax."

No. Not a chance. I hear the doubters. I know what they say. They say it's too late. They say if you don't get recruited out of high school, it's not happening. Nobody walks on to a D3 and goes anywhere after that, unless you already had a D1 offer and blew it for some reason. I hate to remind them, but I didn't walk on. I got a scholarship. Not a full ride, but partial. I'm getting paid three thousand dollars to make my dream reality, and what I know and they don't know is that a dream is only as strong as the person who believes in it. The second you doubt it, that dream is dead. Let them talk. That's them. This is me. They'll get to know me soon enough.

Lizzy

I had partial offers from some of the best schools in the country, but took the full ride here. This wasn't even one of my safety schools, much less a dream school. I'm not sure I had even heard of them before their relentless stream of brochures started arriving in the mail, but they had no application fee, and they didn't attach any extra sections to the Common App, so I took a minute to fill in their information and submit it, just to see what would happen. I forgot about it until a couple of friends and rivals from my high school were denied entry, which freaked them out and intrigued me. They had only applied to get an acceptance out of the way and gain some confidence before the regular season of notifications started, but instead they ended up sweating and panicking for two months until some of their dream schools came through. Then I noticed a fair number of students with Ivy-league level numbers were whining on the discussion boards about being denied admission as well, which made the offer all the more compelling by the time it arrived. I was more concerned with its size than reputation. Smaller school, fewer connections, that's what kept me from committing until the last day to submit my intent to register, before I decided to take pride in being practical.

Working as a research assistant for Dr. Ulrich has helped cushion the disappointment over what has happened since. Her paper is about the intersection of wealth and merit in the application process. It's a shame wealth and merit are so often mutually exclusive. If I had access to the advantages my classmates squandered, I would have had a full ride to someplace higher on my list, a full ride to a dream. The practical choice would have also been an elite one. Like Dr. Ulrich said, though, not many students get to be a research assistant in their first year. That's the kind of advantage Reyna pitched me in her letters and her phone calls when I was considering my options. She was the admissions officer assigned to me, and she sold the smallness hard. She said I'd be lost in a crowd of class presidents and valedictorians at those big, boastful universities. Here, I'd be a star.

But I'm not sure size had much to do with my promotion to research assistant. I was one of the authors of a campus news article that broke the story of how I ended up in a class of rich, functionally-illiterate meatheads and airheads. I use both terms because I think of meatheads as male, and airheads as female. The size factor may even come back to haunt me. Our story was picked up by some major news outlets, and one bad year can drop the ranking of a school our size to a large degree. Dr. Ulrich said I'll be able to transfer to just about any school after my sophomore year, however, based on my involvement in these projects. By studying and reporting on the very thing that may tank the school's reputation, I'll be able to go to a better one. Even more ironic, I doubt I'll be interested in going.

Our scandal was dubbed "Snotgate" after it splashed into the mainstream. Not by any journalist. Someone used it in a comment thread, and it stuck. It's of course a tribute to the rich snots involved, and the lazy legacy of adding "gate" to the end of any nickname hung on a scandal in honor of Watergate. Water had nothing to do with Watergate, it's just the name of a hotel, so why doesn't anyone ever use the first part of the name? I want our scandal to be called "Watersnot". Not just to play with the cliché, but because the behavior of my classmates was not as salacious as everyone wanted it to be. People wanted sludge, but it was only water. They wanted hammocks with holes in the middle and furry costumes with cocaine sprinkled on them like dandruff. All I found was alcohol, loud music, hookups, and hangovers. Which was a relief, as far as I was concerned. Behavior that was too outlandish would have distracted from the real story. The point isn't how many ways they could fill a kiddie pool, or what the hole in the hammock was for, the point is that they were granted admission in the first place. Every student I hung out with in high school could recite their GPA out to three decimal places. When I asked our notorious first-years about their high school GPA, their standard answer was either "two-something" or "three-something." But they could recall every detail of the depravity they were getting into with their newfound subsidized freedom.

The seniors on the news staff who interviewed the admissions officers had it easy. The people in admissions felt guilty. They said they got high on rebellion and lied to themselves. The people I had to interview were still lying to themselves, and I think they might never stop.

I tried to be sympathetic, thinking maybe they were living like they had a lobotomy because their senior year was snatched away and stuck online, but I learned a lot of them were from districts where the only signs of a pandemic were a few teachers and secretaries wearing masks, and those who did come from severe districts didn't seem to have let that get in the way of their partying. They were Advanced Placement partiers, well-prepared for the next level. Another way I tried to give them the benefit of the doubt is wonder if it was me, if I needed to loosen up. But what they do is such a bore. Maybe I'd be interested if their antics were truly depraved, instead of merely unhealthy, and an affront to people trying to pay rent and put food on the table. Their lives are not the bright-colored energy drinks they think they are. It's only water. They think it's something more because they've never done it before.

"Watersnot," Brie repeated to herself and giggled.

"I'm really proud of that," I said. "I wish I could make it happen."

We sat on each end of my bed scrolling through our phones, dressed in our jammies, our feet touching.

"Write a follow-up," she suggested. "Previously unreleased tales of decadence from Covid College."

"Making them sound decadent would require way too much artistic liberty."

I put my phone down and stretched.

"Thank you for not making so much noise when you stretched this time," she said.

"Do I make a lot of noise when I stretch?"

"Almost as much noise as when you yawn."

"Sorry," I sounded defensive.

"I'm changing your life for the better," she played defense with me.

"Well, then use Watersnot every chance you get," I said. "Discord servers, comment threads, conversations. Let's do this."

Brianna is why I don't think I'll be interested in transferring anytime soon. I'd call her my best friend, but I feel like it's too soon. I believe I need to know someone for years before calling them a best friend. So instead I call her my best friend yet.

She was one of my fellow first-years that I interviewed for the article. We were in Psychology together Fall semester. By her own admission, she's not a good student, which is of course why I talked to her. But her badness was a different kind of bad. She wasn't disinterested, she was overwhelmed. I hadn't really considered that version of a bad student before. I was so bent on chasing down the ones who were terrible due to lack of effort, I failed to realize maybe some of them wanted to be good, but weren't prepared to be for whatever reasons.

If I ever do write a follow-up to the scandal-breaker, it will be about Brie, and others like her.

She has a learning challenge. That's all I'm going to call it. Neither of us knows what it is, exactly. I have some ideas based on the research I've done, but I'm not qualified to make a diagnosis. She's in the process of meeting with a specialist who works at a nearby community college. They don't have that kind of specialist on staff here, but they gave her the referral. I'm proud of her for following through on it, since I had a hard time persuading her to make the first appointment on our campus.

Her parents don't believe anything is beyond a person's control. Their families came from a culture where there were too many other things to worry about. People had no time for disorders or disabilities. Those are luxury items. There was shelter to maintain and people to feed. Building a business in the United States was nothing compared to what their families had to do. Her parents knew how fortunate they were to attend school. Their daughter was even luckier. But like a lot of lucky people, she was lazy. That's what they thought. If Brie was struggling in school, they reasoned, it was because she didn't try hard enough.

"My grandparents told my parents don't chase the American dream," she told me when our friendship started to go deep. "Dreams fail. Sell the dreamers what they need for their chase. Don't be the gold miners, be the owners of the hardware store."

Her job as the next generation was to take the next step.

"Be the person they all come to with their problems," she quoted what her parents had in mind for her. "Legal problems, medical problems, logistical problems. Whatever problem you have the talent to solve."

She didn't have that kind of talent. She spent so much time in tutoring, just trying to pass her classes, she wasn't sure what her talents were. She liked to dance, but her parents only allowed her on a dance team to sweeten her college applications. She was never a strong member of the team, anyway, since she couldn't dedicate enough time to perfect the moves. She liked animals, and volunteered at a shelter, but that would always be the extent of it. She might be able to pass an anatomy class, but anything beyond that in pursuit of veterinary science would be out of reach. Besides, her parents said vets weren't real doctors.

I told her we should swap parents. Mine were angered by my ambition. They liked to tell people how many generations their family had lived in our hometown, because that's all they had going for them. They took pride in a legacy of failure. My determination to break the cycle offended them.

"They would love a daughter who taught dance at the rec center and worked as a receptionist at the humane society," I told her. They would love that daughter more than they could express, because one thing they have in common with her parents is they only know how to express frustration.

Brie and I have been working out a plan to visit each other's families during one of our breaks. We're thinking she'll come with me for winter break, and I'll go with her for spring break. Summer break would be too long for anyone involved. My folks would fawn over Brie, her folks would fawn over me, but we wouldn't be jealous of one another. We would grow tired of being fawned over.

Our classmates would love it. They can't seem to get enough fawning. They tell each other all the time how awesome they are. Or how lit or dope they are. They'll often put a "crazy" or a "super" in front of whatever word they use, and a "for real" afterwards, so they become crazy awesome or super dope, for real. Their handful of words have no meaning, they use them so often. They have taken that handful and clenched it into a fist, squeezed out the life, and created zombie words that roam aimlessly through every description. They use their undead handful to describe the crepe bar in the dining hall, weed, any song that makes their head bob, hard seltzer, the beach, the ability to shotgun a can of hard seltzer, everything, including friendship. But they never tell each other they're super awesome for real when sober, only when crazy drunk.

Brie and I are not afraid of silence. I knew our friendship was strong when I was comfortable being quiet around her. That's something I've heard is important in marriage. The research on friendship is less clear. Everyone wants to study romance. Academics, artists, journalists all see romance as undefinable, so they claim whatever they want and their work finds an audience. Friendship is taken for granted. People have more friends than lovers, so they wonder less about them. I wonder quite a bit about my future with Brie, as confident as I may be about it, but haven't found much in the college databases about friendship that's very useful. If we were romantic, I'd have more than enough information, probably too much. Maybe that's why we don't fret over friendship, because we're not coached into overthinking it.

I'm proud of basing my potential transfer on a friend, something that matters, rather than rankings and metrics and money, all the things that guided my previous major life decision. True, that choice led me here, and I found Brie in this field of halfwits, but the chain of events has me thinking everything is random. And if all is left to chance, I might as well make decisions based on the big picture rather than by the numbers. Not that I don't have concerns. I worry if I might be friends with Brie so I can feel superior to someone who had it all when they were growing up and still can't pass me in a race to the top, and if Brie might be friends with me to prove she's not an elitist who looks down on people like me.

"If I was more like our classmates, I wouldn't worry about friends," I thought out loud. "I'd know there would always be people who want to be my friend."

We had been sitting in silence for half an hour before I spoke, each of us in our own thoughts, on each end of my bed, but my sudden speculation didn't take her by surprise.

"But you'd never know who your real friends are," she said, as though she was also writing notes in her phone on the same subject wondering, as I was, where we were and where we were headed.

"That probably wouldn't bother me," I countered. "If I was like them."

"Probably," she agreed for a moment. "Maybe. But you'll never know what it's like to be them."

She put her phone down and bent forward as if reaching for her toes, but beckoned me to take her hands instead. I grasped them and she pulled me back in her direction, then I pulled her back in mine. We went back and forth like that for a while, grunting more than necessary and laughing about our exaggerated effort.

*Dr. Emory Withers*

The conference room was four doors down the hall from my office. I was glad I didn't have to walk from one building to another. I can't take ten steps on campus without someone greeting me, or pulling me aside, and I didn't want to keep the people who were in the conference room waiting for very long. I've found that when expecting a heated meeting, it's best not to let them stew. I was expecting heat, because that's all I had felt since the story broke, so I wanted to get the jump on them. They were some of the most powerful parents of the incoming class, the kinds of families we hope become donors, and if any of them, much less all of them, decided to withhold their support, whatever gains we made thanks to our tuition hack would be a pyrrhic victory.

In our defense, I had inspiring anecdotes ready to share. Before the semester even started, I asked our faculty and staff to be on the lookout for uplifting evidence of our successful return. I didn't single out the incoming class. The call went out as a general request. I didn't want to raise suspicions before they arrived. They deserved a chance to establish their reputation without any preconceptions greeting them. As the examples trickled in, I didn't disregard any delightful stories about the other classes. They served a useful purpose. My bulletin wasn't a complete lie. We did put together a public relations push about our return to campus. But I did have a file set aside for the first-years, and that file remained empty for most of the fall semester. I only managed to gather some contents after their infamy spread beyond our borders and I could be upfront about the need for damage control.

Their welcome week before the first day of classes teased us with hope. They responded well to games and prizes, with more enthusiasm than any group of students before them, as far as any of us could recall. The problems started when the work started. During the early weeks, when I was still gauging how far they could exceed our fears, the only report I could classify as positive, if I squinted hard enough, came from a professor who was amazed at how well they were able to maintain a 2.0 grade point average.

"Like an instinct," she described it as we walked together across the pedestrian bridge from the parking lot one morning. "They seem to have an internal clock, an ultradian rhythm that lets them know exactly how little they need to do in order to get the minimum grade necessary to stay off academic probation."

I decided not to use that one.

Eventually I received a few other options, which was a disappointing sum, but all I needed. Anecdotes can only go so far before a pivot to the trend they supposedly illustrate becomes necessary. There was the student with a previously-undiagnosed learning disability who was not admitted to any other universities, but was thriving in our care. That was my favorite. The other stories involved the superlative work being generated by our honors students. They were full-ride scholars, but I wasn't going to share that unless asked. They were first-year students who would fit right in at any top ten school in the country, which is all that mattered.

The most important point I planned on making is that our plan worked. Our finances were stable after a year of pondering our demise. I had an anecdote of my own to demonstrate how close we came to closing.

During our second Zoom meeting of our first fully-online semester, when we were losing batches of students per day, the board of trustees asked me to devise an exit strategy. I was interested in exploring a merger with the nearest state college, or with the community college district we resided in, but they waved that off as "my thing". They were more interested in selling off real estate. Our conversation was headed for the same impasse as any argument people have over what happens after we die, so I focused on their interests to keep the peace. I asked Terrence, our head of Maintenance and Operations, to set up an appointment with a general contractor to tour the campus and help us see which pieces would be most appealing to a real estate developer, and how those sites could be converted to other uses to help promote their sale.

Terrence was unavailable to make the tour when the day arrived. Something came up. I suspected it was a job interview, though he stammered through an excuse I can't remember because I stopped listening once I knew he was lying. Not that I blamed him. Asking someone to host a meeting dedicated to the elimination of their job is asking more than a lot. He said the contractor would meet me outside the entrance to the pool. He didn't provide a name. He just said "the contractor".

The contractor and I spotted each other at twenty paces. If he had been wearing a mask, which he wasn't, I still would have recognized him. I swear I could hear Terrence laughing, wherever he was. If I knew where, I would have called and ruined his interview before those twenty paces were up.

Conrad Martell was an excellent contractor. I would never deny that. He had won the bid on dozens of jobs for us. His work was impeccable and came in at a fair price. Most of our classrooms that had been reconfigured to accommodate technology upgrades, and all of our walkways that had been redirected to accommodate infrastructure upgrades, were thanks to Conrad. Not reflected in his bids were the costs associated with him blasting right-wing talk radio while he worked. His listening preferences served as bait for passersby, and during his first couple of jobs certain faculty members were lured into heated wastes of time that I had to mediate. We started to send out a memo whenever we hired him encouraging faculty and staff not to engage, and to announce the same recommendation to their students. Every so often a student couldn't resist lingering by the work site and playing their music louder than his talk radio, but they were savvy about moving on when he approached them, so rather than hear from people on our end, I fielded a lot of complaints from Conrad about freedom, liberty, and rights.

"I figured we'd start here," he said when I reached the pool gate. "This and the rec center are the easiest to move. The city or the county would swoop, maybe a private gym franchise, but the government's been screwing them out of existence. Either way, these plots are a quick sell, and they'll hardly need any work."

"Hello, Conrad."

"Oh, sure."

"What?"

"Now I'm the asshole. I didn't think you cared."

"I don't. But that's just what people do. They greet each other."

"There you go," he shook his head. "Never miss a chance to talk down to someone."

A nearby preschool was using the pool while we were on lockdown. The kids were laughing and screaming. It was hard to tell a scream from a laugh.

"I know how they feel," I muttered.

"What did you say? I can't hear you with that mask on."

"Never mind. Let's get this over with."

We moved on to more complex projects. I took simple notes as we walked through empty buildings and he discussed walls, where to add them, where to remove them. We stood in various spots on campus and he pointed to places where fences may need to be built, or taken down, or where a wall would be more effective than a fence. The mental notes I took were much more elaborate. I had not let myself become nostalgic until that day, there was too much to worry about. Touring my abandoned professional home in a mask, as if it was a toxic waste site, removed any restraints on my memory and kept me quiet, which unnerved Conrad.

"Are you gonna say anything?" Conrad barked during our last leg, a quick stop by the dorms, which he had told me easily convert to apartments.

"Sorry," I jotted down *dorms easily convert to apartments* and closed my notebook.

"I've spent most of the years I've known you wishing you would shut up. Now you're freakin' me out. Are you okay?"

"Fine," I assured him for a second before backtracking. "Well..."

I stopped myself. I had made him uncomfortable enough already, and wasn't sure what to say, anyway. The dorms were on a bluff overlooking much of the campus. I removed my mask and breathed in the view. We were far enough apart, and had reached the end of our time together.

"It's tough," he said, sounding much more understanding than I would have expected.

We stood between the first-year and upper-division dorm complexes. One of my earliest decisions twenty years ago had been to position the two groups next to each other so that older students could mentor younger ones. I'm not sure how often that ever happened, but it sounded good on the website.

"Tough," he said again, because he didn't care for being quiet.

"I've been here two decades," I wasn't sure Conrad wanted to hear my thoughts, but silence wasn't working for him, so I went ahead and broadcast them. "Most administrators don't stick around long, wherever they are. If they're a Dean, they want to be a Vice President; if they're a Vice-President, they want to be a President; if they're at a no-name school, they want a name; and above all else is burnout. The job stretches you in a bunch of different directions, and even though you know it's not going to be any different at the next stop, it's a fresh start."

I didn't hear Conrad sigh or grumble, so I proceeded.

"I knew when I got here, this was it. This was the place. I knew I loved it because when I spoke with other presidents and met them at conferences, I never felt like complaining. I had just as many problems to deal with as they did, but it didn't bother me that much. I became a president earlier than I expected, so I had a chance to play the game and apply to some bigger names, but I never wanted to, never even considered it. I know a lot of people think I'm too closely identified with the college, and it's too closely identified with me. But I can't help it. I'm in love."

I looked up at each building, then down at a barbecue we always use to grill hot dogs and hamburgers for the first-year welcome week. I tried to think if we ever used it for anything else, but really kept staring at it to avoid looking at Conrad.

"I'm rooting for you," I heard him say.

"You are?" I looked to make sure it was him.

"Some of my best jobs have been here. There's people to talk to, even if they annoy me sometimes, and you're never late on a payment. Even if all these parcels get bought and there's all these different people who might need work done, I like having everything under one roof. One big cash cow instead of a bunch of little ones."

I appreciated his analogy with a near-laugh.

"I think college is a waste of time," he kept on, "and I've told you so."

"Frequently," I confirmed.

"But at least you guys are private. The kids here don't waste my tax money."

A brief explanation of the federal student loan program would have killed the moment, so instead I teased him with my preferred exit strategy, merging with a state university or community college. He appeared cautiously horrified at the prospect.

"If you do that, if you merge," he wanted clarification, "you'll be public, they won't be private."

"Correct."

Conrad inflated his cheeks and exhaled.

"We'll be able to pay you more," I piled on.

His exhale morphed into a moan of mock agony.

It may have been real agony. It happened over a year ago, and like any memory, it's rewritten on the fly every time I tell it.

The half-dozen parents in the conference room laughed at my most recent draft, which signaled the end of my presentation.

As their laughter subsided, I placed a mental wager on who among them would be the first to speak. I went with Ken Mullins, and won my imaginary bet. He had already put a daughter through our school, and now his son was in his first year. Ken seated himself in the center of the line of parents that faced me, so even if I had never met him before, he was the smart money play.

"That's funny, Spoon," he said as a prelude to whatever else he was going to say.

"Spoon?" one of the two mothers in attendance asked.

"First time I met Emory," he explained as though I wasn't in the room, "I teased him about the name Withers. Kind of an unfortunate name for a leader, isn't it?"

He brought me back into the conversation to play the part of myself in the story he was telling.

"That's what you asked," I played along, but didn't retell the story of my name, since I figured he wanted to do that.

"Spoon explained that when his family first came to America, their full name was Witherspoon, but they decided to shorten it on the documents, so they went with Withers. I said they should've gone with Spoon."

The cohort laughed.

"I guess they couldn't speak English very well," one of fathers chimed in.

"They were English," Ken chided him.

"Just not very smart," I defused any tension.

That sustained their laughter for a few more seconds.

"You've got the touch, Spoon," Ken took the lead again. "Never lost it through this whole shitstorm."

"Thank you, Ken. And I assure you, all of you, we'll get back on track. Like I've been telling anyone who calls for a statement, this was just an emergency measure. When you're faced with selling off your assets, or disappearing into a merger, you get creative."

The parents glanced at one another and shifted in their chairs. Pleasantries were over. The cushion now in place, I braced myself for the blow.

"There seems to be a misunderstanding here, Spoon," said Ken.

I offered an inquisitive expression but kept quiet.

"We appreciate that you have to talk to the media to justify what you did," he proceeded. "And to all those people getting all worked up over it. And you're doing a great job. Your argument is tight. But you don't have to justify anything to us."

I grew even more quietly inquisitive.

"We love what you're doing," the other mother jumped in.

"And we want you to keep doing it," Ken concluded with a reassuring grin.

I didn't know what to say.

Ken did.

"We're not the only ones. Word is spreading among our friends whose kids are at other schools, or looking into where they want to go. There's a niche you can fill here. A pipeline of donors who appreciate that you've stripped away all the bullshit those other colleges pander to. You're never going to catch up to the elite universities. You can't diversify your way up that ladder."

I felt a need to say something. None of my colleagues were in the room, but I owed it to them to try and push back.

"The reason we try to diversify is that studies show college is more of a boost for those in the lower economic rungs than for those in the higher rungs. We're creating a more equitable society, not just a diverse college."

"And the reason they get that boost is because they network with kids like ours," Ken countered. "Brains and ideas are nothing without money behind them. So yeah, let a certain number of them in. Like that girl who wrote the article. If they've earned their way, give them a chance. They deserve it. And what an opportunity it'll be. Instead of going to school with a bunch of other kids trying to make the jump, they'll be going to school with a bunch of kids who can help them. It's the way college really works, only more so."

"And more honestly," said a father who had yet to say a word.

"It's why those idiots paid that con artist half a million dollars to get their kids into college," said the man who thought my English family may not have spoken English well. "They wanted a guarantee. You can provide that."

I reverted back to silence. They were not going to hear themselves, no matter what I said, so I sat back to see how much wider they wanted to dig the trench around their world. I thought maybe some of the others would have more to say, but they had apparently decided Ken was in charge of the shovel.

"On the subject of idiots," he fell back on his reassuring grin again. "We know our kids have had their moments this year. Kids screw up. And college offers them a place to do it safely. A lot of schools have lost sight of that. We appreciate that you haven't. Dropping a steamer in the sand trap off the eighteenth green is stupid, but not worth jeopardizing anyone's future."

"It was the thirteenth," I corrected him. "And it was in the hole."

Everyone tried to suppress their laughter, in part due to the subject matter, but also because they couldn't tell whether Ken was okay with being corrected.

He took a while to unveil his reaction.

"It's not often the real story is better than the one that gets passed around," he said with enough levity to permit the laughs. "But the point stands. We're grateful this is a place where our kids can grow and thrive, without all the pressure of those other places that take themselves too seriously."

They all settled down and agreed with Ken's stance by nodding, each at their own pace. I knew none of them would extend any grace to kids who make mistakes out of desperation rather than on a dare.

I wished some of my more pugnacious colleagues were there with me. Diego would have been perfect. He would have said something incisive and invasive. My career depended on diplomacy. If I was ever good at confrontation, I had long since lost that ability.

Then again, responding too aggressively in the moment would eliminate any chance to entertain what the parents had in mind. There's something to be said for not shooting down a proposal before having a chance to consider it. They may have presented their case in a rather crass manner, but it's important not to let the cosmetics of a presentation distract from the point itself. Any good critical thinker understands that. Maybe it was best Diego wasn't there. He could always talk me out of it later, if I took it that far. I wasn't completely opposed to the idea. What's the old expression? Necessity is the mother of invention? Having our backs against the wall might have led to some sharp insight. If we institutionalize what we did, our acceptance rate would keep shrinking while the revenue would grow. That's the kind of metric that would start turning heads. We could then increase our enrollment, let in more students once the acceptance rate reached a magic number. Some faculty and perhaps some staff would be upset, maybe even resign. But academic jobs, particularly teaching, are hard to come by. We have so much going for us that would appeal to strong candidates.

We're near a vibrant city.

The weather is nice.

It's such a lovely campus.

# Chaos
# (a short story)

Clifford's daughter, Debra, eats a bowl of cereal for dinner while standing at the kitchen counter. She missed the family meal thanks to her late arrival from Homework Club, a program she participates in at her high school because she has fallen rather far behind in her classes. She blames her struggles on the lack of inspiration provided at Harding High School, which is Clifford's alma mater as well. As a point of comparison, she mentions that Melville High School is about to close their computer lab since they are furnishing each of its classrooms with a rack of laptops that can be used during instruction at each teacher's discretion. Clifford asks her what Melville is going to do with their old computers.

"Give them to our school," she says, snorting with contempt through her mouthful of Kix.

Clifford manages to keep quiet, as he doesn't want to give his daughter any more ammunition for her anti-Harding campaign. But later when he and his wife, Lana, are in their room getting ready for bed, he lets fly.

"Nothing's changed since we went to Harding," he complains.

"We didn't have computers back then, Cliff," she says.

"I'm talking about Melville High," he snaps. "Like those kids don't already have their own laptops; the rich just keep getting richer. If it's not gadgets, it's a football stadium, or a pool, or a library. Not to mention that goddamn radio station."

It is the radio station which bothers him the most, for it is the radio station that never lets him forget who's boss, or, more specifically, where the bosses come from. The owner of the trucking company that Clifford drives for is always recalling out loud what a great experience it was for him to host his own radio show at age sixteen. Clifford remembers *Johnny Rocks It*. He remembers hearing a squeaky-voiced kid who could make thirty seconds between songs seem like hours, as he would stammer and hem his way through even the most basic information about what just played and what was to come. And if he tried to tell a joke or drop some knowledge, it could induce tension sweat in the listening audience. Clifford and his buddies used to get drunk and tune it in for a good laugh. Now, all he can say to his boss is, "Wow, that must have been some show."

Clifford also remembers losing to Melville in every sport, every year, for four years. He remembers reading in the local paper about how many Melville graduates were going off to Ivy League schools the following fall. And, thanks to the magic of radio, Melville High will haunt him long after his daughter has graduated from Harding, where those who cannot afford a Melville education end up.

True, he doesn't have to listen. During his morning shift, he doesn't even have to worry about being tempted, since the station broadcasts the BBC World network and National Public Radio while the kids are in class. But for some inexplicable reason, he cannot resist letting the dial linger on Radio Melville for a while during his afternoons behind the wheel of a truck.

"That was Three Doors Down with 'Kryptonite' here on *The Tammy and Tara Show*," announces a young girl with the same teenage accent that Clifford hopes his daughter will lose as she grows older, "and before that was...was...Third Eye Blind?"

"Blink 182, you dork," cackles the other girl.

"Whatever, then...Blink 182, and...we're gonna be playing a lot more oldies for you guys out there."

Clifford groans. Oldies? He was in his thirties when those songs were hits.

"I can't believe you didn't know Third Eye Blind from Blink 182."

"So, that was a long time ago."

Clifford sighs. A long time ago?

"Well, there's like, all these numbers in their names...like, the number three, and third."

"And 182."

"And then one has blink in it and the other is blind, so there's, like, all this stuff with eyes going on."

"Eyes and numbers, yeah, I never really noticed that."

"I know, right? So shut up already."

"You shut up. What does the name have to do with what they sound like? That's like, totally different."

"It's totally not totally different. They rock out, they have names that sound the same, so you should still shut up."

"No, you shut up."

Clifford snaps off the radio. "Money well-spent," he mutters to himself as he pulls into the loading area behind a huge franchise grocery store. He has a brief argument with the manager of the store about what time the shipment was supposed to arrive.

"Corporate's on my ass," the manager tells him.

"They're on everybody's ass," Clifford says. "I'll be sure and bring some tissue next time." He looks around and doesn't see anybody getting ready to unload the shipment. The manager is walking away. "Hey," he calls out to the manager, "where is everybody?"

The manager turns. "We're in the process of hiring some new guys."

"Well, then who's gonna unload this?"

"Who do you think?"

Clifford can't believe this. "What are you talking about? This is *your* store."

"Yeah, so I got things to do."

"And I don't?"

The manager looks over at the full load in the back of Clifford's truck, shrugs, and starts to walk away again.

Clifford catches up to him and looks him in the eye. "You don't know how to drive a forklift, do you?"

The manager smirks. "No, I don't."

"What if I don't, either?"

The manager smiles. "I think you do," he says, and resumes his abandonment of the loading area.

Clifford tries so hard to contain his anger that he starts to shake and has to walk off his frustration. He takes a deep breath and then calls the dispatch office on his cell phone to tell them what's going on. They tell him to go ahead and unload the truck himself. He asks them why, and they tell him it's because the manager isn't really a manager, but some new regional director who's spending time in the trenches as part of his training before he earns his official appointment. The trucking company doesn't want to offend the wrong person and end up losing the account. Clifford ends the call and stares back at the forklift. Once he feels emasculated enough to make his surrender complete and his mood sufficiently calm, he climbs on board and starts it up.

On the drive home, he catches the last part of *The Tammy and Tara Show*.

"So, anyway, the show's about to end, and...oh, yeah...um, Melville High is having their annual Salvation Army drive, and, so, if you've got some, like, old clothes and stuff, bring them to the back of the auditorium this Saturday, 'cause I guess there's a lot of pretty needy people out there, so...it's a kinda good thing to get involved with."

"And some of the clothes are pretty awesome, too."

"Totally, and, like I said, it's a really good cause, so...just be cool and bring some stuff, okay? Okay. This last song is dedicated to our cross country coach..."

"Tammy!"

"What?"

"I'm so sure."

"What? Oh, my God...yeah...and speaking of sports..."

"The football game, Tammy."

"Hullo? That's what I'm saying. I mean, what other sport is there right now besides cross country and football?"

"Okay, then. Excuse me, Miss...Miss...I dunno."

"Whatever...anyway, this Friday night there's a game at Harding, so...everyone come out and watch us kick Harding's butt, as usual..."

Clifford snaps off the radio, and tries to remember the last time he was able to listen to that station without snapping off the radio.

Over dinner, Clifford asks Debra what time the football game starts on Friday.

"Why, you going?" she asks him.

"I was thinking about it."

"They're gonna kick our ass."

Clifford and Lana both tell their daughter to watch her mouth. Lana then reminds Clifford that he gave up going to the Harding-Melville game years ago at the suggestion of their family doctor.

"Yeah, I know, I know," he admits, "but we've got a good team this year, don't we Deb?"

Debra shrugs. "I don't know."

"That's what I read in the paper, sweetie. They're undefeated."

"They haven't played Melville yet, Dad."

"Well..." Clifford realizes that he's about to yell and settles down. "Well, maybe this year will be different."

***

Harding scores to tie the game with just a few minutes left. A few minutes, however, seems to be more than enough time for Melville to put together a winning drive. Harding's defense looks tired.

"Of course they do, dear," says Lana. "They've been playing their hearts out."

"Yeah, yeah, I know." Clifford realizes he doesn't sound very sympathetic. His wife frowns at him. He manages to smile at her.

Looking back from their front-row seat near the far end of the bleachers by the goal line, he sees that the Harding fans look tired, too, like they put up a good fight for a while, but realize that Melville is destined to win again. He spots Debra at the top of the bleachers with a group of girls. They're passing around a pair of binoculars to pick out the best-looking boys on the Melville sideline.

"What's wrong with *our* boys?" Clifford says out loud.

"Like I said, dear, they're tired," says Lana.

He thinks about explaining to his wife what he really meant, but decides not to waste any energy he could be using to help defeat the enemy. It doesn't appear as though anything he can do will help, however, as a Melville player has broken free from the pack at the fifty-yard line and is running untouched towards the end zone.

He stands up and hollers at the top of his lungs, "Stop him! Stop him! Godammit, stop him!"

Everyone around him is on their feet, yelling more or less the same thing. The Melville player runs to the thirty-yard line, the twenty-five, the twenty...

"Stop him! Stop him!"

Clifford can't control himself. Without a second thought, he jumps over the railing in front of the bleachers and sprints across the running track towards the field. He hears nothing, he sees nothing, except the Melville ball-carrier dashing towards the goal line. The Melville player is about to pass the Harding reserve players standing along the sideline. Clifford runs towards the empty space between the last Harding reserve and the goal line. As the Melville player passes by the opening, Clifford has an angle on him. A few yards shy of the sideline, Clifford dives through the air. He nails the Melville player around the five yard line, driving him into the turf. He sits up, keeping the kid pinned beneath his knees. The kid looks up at him and screams, "What the fuck is going on!?"

"You can't always get what you want, kid."

"Who the hell are you?"

"I'm the unexpected," he grabs the kid by the face mask. "I'm chaos."

Several Harding players are pulling Clifford off the kid before the security guards have a chance to get there. The guards are not needed, however. He willingly gets off the kid and walks back towards the bleachers. He assures each person who rushes him that he's okay, that he doesn't want any trouble. He has already caused quite a bit of trouble, though. Bombarded with faces and voices, Clifford finally spots his wife standing in the front row. She doesn't seem to be able to move any muscles in her face. She leaves.

"Wait," he tries to run towards her, but there are too many people surrounding him. He yells a few more times for her to wait, but he is stuck in the middle of the crowd.

***

"They gave him the touchdown," Lana says to him the following morning. He is sprawled out on the couch, having arrived late last night to a locked bedroom door.

Clifford rubs his eyes. "That's what I heard."

"They tell you that at the police station?" she asks.

Clifford hesitates. He had called Lana from the station last night to bail him out. Her only words to him had been, "See you in the morning. Good night."

"Yes," he says, "I heard about it last night."

She still doesn't know what to say to him. He doesn't know what to say to her, either, other than "I'm sorry."

"I'm not so sure I can accept your apology right now," she sighs.

"I know, I know."

"And as for your daughter..."

"I know."

"Then why did you do it?"

He cannot sort through all the reasons. "It was just a feeling," he says.

Lana stares at him for a while. She's breathing pretty heavily. Finally, she asks him if anybody's going to press charges.

"No. They got in touch with the kid's family and they weren't interested, so they let me go." He looks over at the door to his daughter's room. "Is she home?"

Lana nods her head. "Yes, but I wouldn't try saying you're sorry to her for a while. I wouldn't even try to talk to her for a while."

He understands perfectly. If he waits long enough, he thinks, his daughter will know how he feels, and he won't have to explain himself. That's going to take some time, though. For his daughter's sake, he hopes it takes a long time. Maybe she'll even marry one of those Melville boys she was admiring through the binoculars last night.

Clifford has a cup of coffee with his wife, and goes to work. It feels like just another Saturday.

At the motor pool he climbs into the driver's seat of the truck, and turns the ignition. The radio is still set on Radio Melville.

A soothing, low-pitched male voice with a British accent glides from the speakers. "This is the BBC World Wide Network. Greenwich Meridian Time is now sixteen hundred hours..."

A series of three short beeps is followed by a sustained tone of the same pitch. Radio Melville is now on the air.

"Hi, this is Tammy!"

"And this is Tara!"

(In unison) "And this is the Tammy and Tara Show! Whooo!"

The girls' shrieks seem to resonate up and down Clifford's spine. He grips the wheel tighter and sets his jaw as he pulls out of the lot.

"Welcome to a special Saturday edition of Tammy and Tara. And I'm sure all you guys know why we're doing this."

"Everybody out there catch that game last night?"

"Oh...my...God...who was that man?"

"Oh my God, that was so out of control!"

"That was soooo weird."

Clifford pulls over as soon as he straightens the truck out onto the street. He turns the volume up slightly and leans forward, staring at the radio.

"We have got to get that guy on the show."

"Oh, totally."

"Everyone was coming up to me and telling me that. He is, like, the god of Melville High right now."

"I know, right?"

"I mean, I wanna have kids, just so I can tell them about the time that psycho guy ran out onto the field and tackled Karch before he got into the end zone. That was soooo rad!"

"Oh, and Bailey? If you're listening? Call us and tell us if you got a picture of that for the yearbook?"

"Like, a good one. Not a blurry screen grab from one of those jiggly videos."

"Oh my God, totally. I'm praying to God there is one good picture out there."

"Mr. Psycho Guy? If you're out there, like, listening to the show? We love you!"

"That's right, we totally love you!"

"And we're gonna find you."

"Totally! Come on, listeners! Someone must know someone at Harding who can tell us who he is. Start texting, start posting! We want this guy!"

"It's just a matter of time!"

"I know, right? Mr. Psycho Harding Guy for President!"

"Whoooo!"

Clifford leans back and stares straight ahead, breathing through his mouth. The engine runs. He does not move.

# Focus

# (a short story)

The first time Juliette saw a Great Blue Heron was on a fourth-grade field trip. She still has the watercolor she painted in class afterwards, in response to the teacher's request for everyone to "paint your most vivid memory from our trip to the marshlands." It is now framed and hanging in her office: a big blue cross which could pass for a child's rendition of an airplane, if it weren't for the big orange beak protruding from the nose.

Adulthood and a thousand sightings have not diminished the bird's appeal. Anticipation still jumps her pulse rate each time she approaches one of the likely ponds or reservoirs she has lingered by for years. Sometimes she brings her camera. Sometimes she prefers not to be bothered with a lens between herself and the quiet, slate-colored giants who seem to materialize in the reeds and mist as if they were there all along, waiting to be discovered. They are like totem poles to her, fit for worship in their stillness, in the stealth and patience they exercise in stalking a fish, yet always ready to fly away should an admirer get too close, always keeping their distance and their mystery. Their flight is just as thrilling: legs outstretched at one end, beak spearing through the air from its neck curled slightly at the other, body bouncing between the lanky bow and stern thanks to the pumping of its sprawling wingspan. And the colors: in motion, in waiting...the blue-tinted gray of the body and wings a backdrop, a centerpiece for the orange of the beak, white head crested with a black headdress, white slightly rusting as it blends into the long neck, white quills unfurling at the bottom of the neck, a hint of red at the top of its never-ending legs. As intimidating in the sky as they are silent, noble, and discerning in their movements along the shore, Juliette likes to say that Great Blue Herons are cats on the ground, and horses in the air.

The marsh below the bridge on the way to town offers no herons this morning, so she continues driving to the post office with no excuses to stop. She breathes in the air which enters her open window from the farmlands and forests surrounding her commute, and pities those who continue to live in the city, those who do not take the time to appreciate what is beyond.

The postmaster, her thick head and shoulders just visible above the counter, greets Juliette with a smile and a "Good morning, Ms. Wahl. Have you been working this morning?"

"No," says Juliette, barely making eye contact as she walks to her post office box, "not this morning."

"We've got the new phone books in. One of your pictures is on the cover."

Juliette reaches her box and jimmies the key into the lock. "The old school house, right?"

"That's the one." The postmaster reaches below the counter and plops the book on the desk with a satisfying thud. She seems proud to know Juliette, who is more interested in what's inside her box.

"Yes. They told me they liked that one," Juliette offers as she sifts through the mail in her hand.

"Well, I like it, too," says the postmaster. "My husband works for the phone company, and he told everyone at work I know you."

"That's nice of him."

"He's about the only one who works in this region, but a couple times a week he needs to run up to headquarters, you know, so that's when he sees all those other guys."

"I see."

The postmaster hesitates. Juliette can sense that she is watching her. "You know, Ms. Wahl," she says, finally.

"Yes?" Juliette has given up focusing on her mail, but still pretends to be doing it.

"I don't mean to pry, but I notice you get a lot of things from the IRS."

Juliette looks up at her. The postmaster raises her hands as though Juliette has drawn a gun. "I don't mean to pry, like I said, we just have a lot of respect for you, my husband and me, and I thought maybe you were in some sort of trouble. I was only telling him about your mail because it really bothered me. I was concerned. Like I said, I don't mean to pry; I just want to make sure you're okay and everything..."

"I work for them." Juliette admits.

"Ohhhhh," says the postmaster. "Thank goodness...but what a surprise. So many of the people who live around here are retired or artistic types, you know, besides the farmers, of course, so I just assumed you made a living off your pictures."

"I'm very choosy," Juliette shoots back. "I do a lot of exhibits, which don't really pay."

"That's wonderful," the postmaster assures Juliette. "I admire a person who sticks to their guns. We could all be a little less money-hungry, really."

"As a matter of fact," Juliette continues, "I have an exhibit coming up in a few weeks which I'm putting together right now." Juliette takes a postcard flyer from her purse and places it on the counter. "It's part of a homeless benefit."

"What a great idea," says the postmaster. "Me and Lowell will really try and make it. Do we have to give any money?"

"No," Juliette barely manages to withhold a sigh. "There's a suggested donation, but it's just a suggestion."

"Oh, okay. Where is this place?"

Juliette wishes she could take the postcard back. "It's a coffee house," she explains to her, "in that little downtown area between here and the main freeway."

"Is there a coffee shop there? It's such a cute little place."

"Not a coffee shop, a coffee house. You know, one of those places with cappuccino and a little bakery?"

"Ohhhh, of course. I was thinking coffee *shop*. That sounds like a lot of fun. I can't wait to tell Lowell. Thank you so much for the invitation," she smiles at Juliette.

"You don't need an invitation," Juliette quickly adds. "Anyone can come."

"Sure, but we wouldn't have known about it," the postmaster beams.

"True," realizes Juliette, "Very true."

Juliette does not feel like sitting at her computer just yet, so she drives into the city to work on her homeless project.

"Could you hold your cup a little higher?" she instructs a man with a cardboard sign asking for change.

"I can't see your tattoo. Pull up your shirt sleeve," she orders a barely-conscious man sprawled out in a doorway.

"Hold the baby there, just below your chin," she positions a woman sitting on the stoop of a condemned building.

***

"I hope our work here tonight provides a legacy of hope for the homeless on our streets," she imparts to the small crowd at the coffee house. "Not only through any money raised here tonight, but through our raised awareness, our raised consciousness. If we are to make the world a better place, it takes more than just pictures on a wall. It takes us. Thank you."

The room fills with applause. Juliette acknowledges it with a slight nod. She searches the room for the postmaster and her husband, but cannot find them. She smiles and nods a little larger.

Having fulfilled her obligation, Juliette returns to her favorite subject in grand fashion. Always going to the birds, she decides to try and have the birds come to her. Wearing a pair of rubber wading pants freshly-purchased from a sporting goods store, she wades into the shallow waters of a pond within the borders of a bird sanctuary frequented by herons, camera in tow, well beyond where people are permitted. She finds a spot in the reeds to camouflage herself from any arriving herons, and from the eyes of any state park rangers who may drive by. The risk of being discovered and forced to pay a fine heightens her sense of adventure. Sitting as still as possible allows her to feel her own heartbeat, to feel her adrenaline charge the nerve endings just below the surface of her skin.

A heron lands just a few yards away from her, to her left slightly, just beyond the reeds. She takes a deep breath, and tries to retrace its flight path: right over her head, apparently. Juliette never saw it coming. The Great Blue Heron extends its neck to its full height, scanning the waters for movement with a slight, graceful turn of its head every so often, while its body maintains an absence of movement which puts Juliette's efforts in waiting to shame. She feels as though she could laugh out loud, she is so delighted to be so close. Trying not to make any noise, she raises her camera. The muscles in her arm shifting cause her back muscles to flex, which run down to her legs and create the slightest amount of friction between them and the rubber wading pants. They groan softly.

The heron swings its neck and smoothly swivels its head in Juliette's direction. She freezes. The heron's eyes never blink, they burn. Juliette feels ashamed. She wishes she could apologize. The heron does not fly away, however. It takes a step towards her. And another. Each step is accompanied by a slight bob of the great bird's neck and head. Juliette's shame turns to awe. She forgets about her camera. She wants to make contact. She stares into the heron's fiery eyes, and holds out her hand, palm facing down, as she was taught to do as a child when introduced to a dog unfamiliar with her scent. The heron behaves accordingly, stretching its neck towards her hand, its beak practically touching Juliette's skin. The expression on her face never changes as the heron's neck suddenly snaps back then forward in a flash. In the same flash, Juliette sees the tip of the beak on the other side of her hand, sticking straight out from her palm. She sees the upper part of the beak buried into the top of her hand. She sees the heron fly away, then the bloody hole through the middle of her hand. She drops her camera and screams.

***

"You should have told me you were doing some remodeling," the postmaster says to Juliette. "Lowell is a wizard with a nail gun."

"Well, you know," says Juliette, struggling to sift through her mail thanks to the heavy bandage wrapped around her hand, "I'm just the type that likes to do things myself. Stubborn, I guess."

"Power tools are nothing to get stubborn with, Ms. Wahl," warns the postmaster. "They're only as safe as the person using it."

"Well, now I know," quips Juliette with a tight grin.

The postmaster points over Juliette's shoulder out the window. "Would you look at that," she says. "That certainly would make a pretty picture, wouldn't it Ms. Wahl?"

A huge migration of swallows is pausing in the trees just outside the post office. Their noise grows louder as waves of them arrive by the second.

"Makes those dusty old cypress look like Christmas trees all of a sudden, eh?" the postmaster narrates. Juliette watches the birds with a hollow feeling in her stomach.

"I don't suppose you have your camera handy with that hole in your hand," she hears the postmaster say.

"No," Juliette nearly whispers. "I can't operate it for a while."

"Tell you what, then," announces the postmaster. "I'll snap a few for you. I'm no artist or anything, but at least it'll give you a little something to remember them by."

The postmaster bounds out of the office with her phone raised and begins snapping shots of the swallows from all angles around the cypress trees. Juliette watches her, then watches the birds, who have no interest in being remembered, and wonders if she could ever be the same.

# Titles With Colons:

## (A Novelette Concerning the Intersection of a Decentralized Media Landscape with the Human Compulsion for Control)

*I. Information Imbalance and Client Confidentiality in the Field of Academic Dishonesty*

My clients prefer not to talk about themselves.

They know as much about me as they want. I never refuse to answer a question. It's an easy oath to pledge because they don't ask many.

I use my real name in our transactions. They usually have a pseudonym, some kind of online handle they use on message boards and comment threads. I've worked for Kayleyfornia, YooTuba, Academiahhh, CleanCole.

I understand. If anyone finds out about our transaction, they're the ones who look bad. I'm the wizard behind the curtain. They're the ones who tried to pass off my words as their own. They didn't follow through on a project based on a subject they supposedly studied for years. I do the work in two weeks: one for studying, one for composing, with an hour, at most, spent looking over samples of their own writing to get a sense of their voice. I often only need about ten minutes to recognize their patterns. Claiming to personalize their style is part of my appeal. Artificial Intelligence and Large Language Models cannot get to know them, the promotion goes, but I can.

I provide them with a product meant to represent what they want to do with their life. Child Psychiatry, Business Administration, Microbiology, Behavioral Economics, Astrophysics, I've done it all. All they've done is cheat. The subject is incidental. What they really want to do with their life is get by. I've told them so in some cases. They feel guilty, and think my fee includes sympathy, so they express remorse.

I tell them that if they really loved their major, they would never let someone else do the work for them. If they really loved it, they would fight through their fear of writing, work hard to learn the concepts that eluded them, and they would not be at all bothered by the likelihood that no one, other than their thesis advisors, is ever going to read what they wrote. Their love of what they do would propel them. Even if they knew there was a strong possibility they would not be able to work in their chosen field, that awareness would make them love the pursuit even more. College is the rare time in life we're guaranteed a chance to do what we love, if only for a moment, if we know what that love is.

Mine was Comparative Literature. I especially enjoyed looking for classical narrative patterns in pop culture. My master's thesis focused on Elvis movies. I demonstrated how many films in the Elvis library served as travel guides for a wide audience in the form of a "Stranger in a Strange Land" template. I relied heavily on *Fun in Acapulco, Blue Hawaii, G.I. Blues,* and *It Happened at the World's Fair* to show how Elvis functioned as an aspirational stand-in for the viewer and provided safe passage to places that many considered exotic at the time. I thought of myself in a similar way as I would start another journey into a new subject I had been hired to learn about, imagining my job was to travel the highways and back alleys of information in search of sources to help guide an audience through an argument.

When I first started ghostwriting, I was surprised at how much you can learn about any subject in a week. As the jobs accumulated, I was surprised at how much you can learn about a person in a minute. Of course, I was always dealing with the same person. The same lazy, entitled person with the same excuses.

"Hello?"

I was genuinely curious who was calling, because no one ever uses their phone to make a phone call.

"I get it," the voice on the other end heard the suspicion in mine. "Shall I text instead?"

"Do I know you?"

"Not yet. It's business."

"Clients don't even text. They email."

"All the more reason to call."

"You're not like other clients," I handled his self-promotion for him.

"I'll prove it."

"This is a ghostwriting job," I assumed.

"You provide other services?"

"Not that one lately. I've been pursuing other projects."

"Writing projects?"

"Yes."

"Good. Because I want to pay you a lot of money, but not if you're rusty."

The ghostwriting experience had turned me to jade.

You may have noticed.

Which is why, with more offers than I could accept, I had decided to make a change.

I wanted to write more creatively, but was still fascinated by fooling people, so I took a job with a web designer who published phony articles designed to go viral within politically rabid circles. My first gig was for a figment of my editor's imagination called the Spokane Argot. The websites all had names that sounded like plausible news outlets. He said if you call your site something like "Freedom Warrior" or "Truth Eagle" you're giving away the game, but a bland brand keeps the focus on the story. If someone wants to check its authenticity, they run with the content rather than its source. Soon enough, before people even finish typing "Clinton", one of the suggestions is "Clinton sex island", which is plenty of confirmation for the converted. Meanwhile, the Tulsa Lamplighter, or the Santa Fe Star-Times, it stays in the shadows. He combined mid-sized cities with impressive titles. If the city was too large, too many people would know too soon that the source was a fabrication, while the title served to remind us how we needed to approach our hoaxes: the more outlandish the events, the more straightforward the reporting had to be. The premise of the story was our chance to be clever. The writing of it had to be dry. Anything that successfully makes the rounds is uncovered at some point, but the longer it goes unnoticed by those who know it isn't true, the more time it has to become fact to those who want it to be true.

"Is there any money in that?" the voice asked.

"He sells ad space on the sites, like any other news outlet."

"Any in it for you?"

"I'm not in it for the money."

"What a waste of your talent."

"It's fun watching the reactions."

"Even though they don't know it's you?"

"Maybe because they don't know it's me."

"That's how a criminal thinks."

"How much did you say you want to pay me to pretend I'm you?"

"I assume you don't believe any of the ideas you're promoting."

"Whatever your offer, I'm starting to think it won't to be enough."

"You have written sound arguments, supported with evidence."

"That nobody reads."

"You want to be a person of influence."

"You want a morally upstanding person to cheat for you."

"What if I told you..."

"I hate that phrase..."

"...that my thesis, our thesis, may very well end up with an audience."

"I'd say the key word is 'may'."

"I haven't told you the subject."

"Let me tell you the subject of my latest work," I beamed with pride. "It's for a local paper in Tucson that we still haven't named. One of their reporters, played by me in perhaps my strongest performance yet, was approached by a former Department of Justice bureaucrat who claims that two months into his presidency, Obama replaced Attorney General Eric Holder with a body double they found playing drums in an Earth, Wind, and Fire tribute band."

"Obama? Isn't that a bit dated?"

"Not for our audience. He's classic rock."

"Why wouldn't he just replace Holder with someone else?"

"Holder discovered something."

"What did he discover?"

"My source doesn't know that part."

"Are you sure?"

"Now you're getting it."

"He might be scared."

"She. That's how I imagine her. She moved to Tucson to disappear, but couldn't live with the secret any longer."

"What did they do to Holder?" the voice wondered more than asked, as if reading the piece already.

"She shudders to think."

"What about his family and friends?"

"The family was well-compensated through a shell company. The friends were ghosted by the double. He was instructed to first alienate himself from them, then gradually stop returning their calls."

"Obama himself wasn't a double?"

"Too far," I shook my head and wondered if he could hear my ear rubbing against the phone. "Conspiracy theorists think of their enemies as masterminds, not imposters. They like to imagine all the strings being pulled. And you need to let them decide what the strings are attached to. I leave plenty of room in my stories for their minds to wander."

The voice disappeared into silence, as though his mind was wandering, maybe reaching an understanding as to why I fell for this kind of writing.

"All writing is a form of trickery," I encouraged him to run with those thoughts I assumed he was having. "What I do lays that bare, and is therefore more honest."

"There's travel involved."

"For your thesis project?"

"Yes," he brushed away my summary and my secrets as though they never happened. "Lots of it. The fun kind. No Marriots, no Hiltons, no conference rooms."

"No enclosed spaces and recirculated air," I joined him in leaving my confession behind.

"Wide open spaces only. The great outdoors. Whale watching, mountain climbing…"

"What exactly is the subject?"

"Whether or not ecotourism is good for the environment."

"And you have an answer already."

"I have a title," he confirms. "*Net Positive: The Effect of Ecotourism on the Environment.*"

"With a colon after 'Net Positive' I imagine."

"What's a thesis project without a colon?"

The only medium that uses colons in the title more than academic papers are movie franchises. Each institution has the same motive: to apply a surface level of creativity to a project that most likely needs all the help it can get. But the wells of inspiration they draw from are on opposite ends of the desert. Hollywood wants to look more profound, so rather than call their sequel *Uncle Sam 2*, they go with *Uncle Sam: Anthem Stand.* University researchers who have been cloistered in labs and libraries want to look more colorful, so rather than call their paper *A Longitudinal Study on the Social Ramifications of Water Fluoridation*, they go with *Open Wide: A Longitudinal Study on the Social Ramifications of Water Fluoridation.*

"Clients always do the field work themselves," I noted. "They like the excuse to travel. It's the writing they hate."

"This kind of travel doesn't suit me."

"Afraid of heights? Open water?"

"I have physical limitations."

"Oh. Sorry."

"Relax. I was born this way. I've had my whole life to come to terms with it."

"Wheelchair?"

"Usually. I'll bust out the crutches on special occasions."

"Travel and guilt. You drive a hard bargain."

"It also provides cover. I can hire you as a research assistant."

I thought of a morning two years earlier, while still in residence for my doctorate. I was sitting at a corner table in a coffee house writing my third paper on Camus, one for each school and each degree program I attended. It was my usual maneuver where I apply his essay "The Myth of Sisyphus" to a book from the class reading list. In this case it was *Mrs. Dalloway* by Virginia Woolf. My claim was that the routine lives weaving through the different perspectives swirling around Dalloway exhibit Camus' notion of purpose. But who gives a shit. The point is that I had my first edition copy of *The Stranger* by my side, a gift from my first undergrad advisor who appreciated my first go-round with Camus, in which I applied his philosophy to the *Aliens* franchise (minus *Aliens 3* and any projects that mixed in The Predator). The book had since served as a good luck charm, my talisman that I kept on the table as I wrote, even when I wasn't whoring out Camus yet again.

"Good heavens!" a male patron with a beard exclaimed as he paused by my table. "Is that what I think it is?"

He was looking at my first edition.

"It is."

"Why in the hell are you leaving it exposed like this?"

"It was meant to be carried around and read, not put under glass."

I had been waiting to provide that answer for eight years, but nobody ever noticed whenever I brought the book out in public.

"Please tell me you haven't highlighted any lines and written notes in the margins," said the words coming from the opening in his feral beard. He wore a short blazer with skinny pants and boxy ankle boots, like a talking heron might dress for a tea party in a children's book.

"I haven't taken it that far," I assured him. "I just carry it around."

"You should buy a baby stroller for it, like people do for their dogs."

I assumed he was joking and laughed. Then he offered to buy the book. I asked him how much and laughed at his reply, because I still thought he was joking. Then he went higher. I sat in stunned silence, which he took as a bargaining tactic. He made another offer, then another; offer after offer, until the price started to exceed my ghostwriting fee, then my tuition.

I finally told him it wasn't for sale. I can't remember how he responded. Maybe he stomped away in a huff, he may have called me a fool. I can't remember exactly what he did because I remember exactly what I was thinking: how remarkable that someone can write something which continues to influence people nearly a century after it was published.

The voice inside the phone was right. I wanted to be a person of influence. Yet I enjoyed my anonymity. I wondered if "influence" was a euphemism for manipulation or control. I wouldn't need a large group, so long as they were passionate about my ideas.

I thought about this as I told the voice that I would take the job he offered me, the one he said may attract some attention.

I gave him my PayPal account information, which served as our handshake. We stopped speaking over the phone. Our correspondence became more typical of my previous clients. We exchanged brief emails. I provided research documentation and pages of a draft. He sent me samples of his unremarkable writing and quite remarkable travel arrangements.

One of the trips involved whale watching in a sprawling lagoon on a remote stretch of the Baja Peninsula. I drove to San Diego and caught a shuttle bus to a small executive airport next to Tijuana International. As we sat in traffic waiting to cross the border, I imagined that if I ever published a book, I would call it *One Book,* as in "If you read one book this year, read this one."

What I thought was a clever play on that old rave review cliché.

Then I happened to see a car with a personalized license plate, or maybe it was a bumper sticker, that was supposed to be funny, and could have been if it wasn't stuck there telling the same joke over and over again. Nothing holds up that well. And that title I was considering would be further proof, stuck on the cover telling the same joke, like a bumper sticker, or a t-shirt browbeating its reader with a clever expression doomed to fade in the wash. "*One Book.* Got it. Thank you. Very funny."

It would also create problems for the colon. If I ever published a book, it would probably be about my addiction to academia, my life as a career student, so I would have to use a colon. If I called my work *One Book*, where would that leave my colon? As a prelude to explain the joke? Or a word orgy summarizing the plot?

*II: The Effect of Condescending Silence on the Career Trajectories of Aspiring Academics*

A written transcript would not reveal the damage. Nobody ever said anything hurtful.

They were silent.

I would raise a point and they would pause. I would hope the silence was a moment of reflection, that they were considering what I said.

They would move on.

Not every time.

But most of the time.

An audio recording might expose the tone of their voices as they emerged from their snotty pause pretending I said nothing, but it was subtle. You had to be there, see their faces.

I should have stopped at a master's degree. I knew the pitfalls of a PhD before I started one. I understood the employment challenges, the debt load, even the possibility of a ruthless environment (though not the quiet kind that suffocated my attempt). But I was better at being a student than anything else I had tried in life, and didn't want to let go of that feeling.

Maybe it was all the time I spent behind espresso machines and deli counters and cash registers staring at the front of the store, out the windows, wanting something more. Not more customers. I preferred an empty stretch to a rush. But more depth underneath the emptiness. The quiet I experienced as a student was so much more profound than the quiet on the jobs I worked to help pay for being a student. My school silence was a space to think. My work silence smelled of raw meat and wet coffee grinds. It left stains on my apron and cap. The best part of that kind of work was when I washed off the results. As a student, I treasured the results of my work.

Only I never felt like a student in the PhD program. More like a private contractor, as if I had been hired to conduct research and write, rather than paying top dollar for the privilege. The discouraging lack of interaction during seminar discussions, those loogies of silence hocked in my face, symbolized the isolation.

Most of my colleagues, and I hesitate to use that word, were already working in in their field, and the PhD was a ticket up and to the right on their company's salary grid. But they weren't the problem. The pros kept to themselves, taking most of their coursework online, arriving for the occasional evening class, and heading home afterwards.

The lifers were the issue. The career academics who hung around campus like aged-out high school hot shots who keep going to the football games, the spring musicals, or whatever their glory days revolved around. They taught courses, but weren't all that interested in teaching. They were into whipping out what they had learned and wagging it around in front of the class, whether it was relevant to the subject matter or not. When students called them "doctor", they never corrected them.

We may as well have been in cubicles, on a trading floor, or at a call center working on commission. Rather than sales, we earned intellectual capital in our quest to be Scholar King of the Pedants. People claim academia is not grounded enough in the real world. They're wrong. The ivory tower is as hard to climb and as slippery as any skyscraper.

I had no goal in mind for when I finished my doctorate. Maybe a nebulous interest in teaching. All I wanted from the future was to walk on warm evenings along a tree-lined street, maybe to get the mail, as long as mail exists. That was my favorite part of my doctoral work. I rented an apartment in a complex that looked like luxury condos. I loved when the sun would set in the late summer and early fall and I walked in shorts and a t-shirt below the leafy branches of the sycamore trees, wrapped in warm air, kids riding bikes and cats rolling on front lawns hoping for belly rubs.

With each August and September walk, my fear of not being able to rise to that atmosphere flourished, so I took the characteristics that my half-completed PhD enhanced, research and writing in isolation, and applied them to a field that valued such a lonely profile.

When I started ghostwriting, I tried to stay on course for my doctorate as long as I could. I thought establishing my own brand rather than working for an essay mill would allow for that balance. Promoting my services was an upfront investment in my business that stole more time than the actual writing of other people's essays, and provided a glimpse of the commitment to come that would overwhelm all other pursuits, including my latest degree.

In researching the best practices of successful ghostwriters, I looked for ways I could adhere to the formula without being too formulaic. The value of repeat customers led to my attempt at a personal touch. I wanted to forge relationships with my clients. I stayed in the college town with the apartment shrouded in trees that I loved to rent. Besides the smallish private university I attended, there was a large state school within a half hour's drive. I took meetings with customers to get a sense of their voice.

I abandoned this idea within a few jobs. The people I met made me want to sabotage their efforts to plagiarize rather than help them get away with it. I wanted to insert a random sentence in the middle of every essay that included a confession and my contact info. The clients never would have noticed. I'm positive they never read the essays I wrote for them. They were spoiled and undeserving of their position in life. They had always been lousy students and got into college because they were able to afford expensive SAT preparation that led to scores which allowed enrollment managers to overlook their mediocre grades, or they played one of those sports favored by rich people that put them on a recruitment list with lower standards than those applied to students who don't play squash. They didn't want to go to college. Their parents wanted them to go, in spite of their children's disinterest and inability. Mom and Dad had a need to namedrop where their kid went, a place that served as shorthand validation of their parenting, and prove their tax bracket wasn't luck, it was genetics. Meanwhile, the kids alternated between pretending deadlines didn't exist, and panicking when they arrived.

I tried using their desperation as a means to sympathize with them, but that didn't work, because they were buying their way out of desperation. After I finished a second paper for the halfwit polo player (the kind with horses, not water), I refused return business from the sort-of-pretty girl who was bored with anything that wasn't on the screen of her phone, and from the international student who needed a degree to take over his father's petroleum exploration company in Saudi Arabia. The oil scion would have a been a strong candidate for pity, given his struggles with a non-native language, if he had not been the most entitled of all the clients I made the mistake of getting to know in those early days. The others benefitted from systemic privilege that was hard to see if you weren't looking for it, whereas the scion from the House of Saud was involved in a blatant quid pro quo with his family, which led him to apply that same transactional dynamic to all of his other relations, including me and the college. I wondered what his dating life was like.

I relented to the standard ghostwriter business model and kept the relationships online. I continued to use my name, while they started to disguise theirs. Rather than concern myself with capturing their written voice, I selected essays that were assigned in large forum classes, where the professors and teaching assistants would not have time to develop a feel for anyone's style.

This emotional distance from the job led me to develop a character whose voice I adopted when I wrote other people's essays. I named the voice "Leslie", since it could apply to either gender. Leslie was a student trying to impress the reader by using vocabulary they would never use in conversation. Usually this was a matter of using *therefore* instead of *so*, and *however* instead of *but*. On occasion it involved consulting the thesaurus and choosing a word from the bottom of the list when it was least necessary. "Why use *explore* when you can use *reconnoiter*?" Leslie would think. "That'll dazzle 'em."

Leslie's transitions from one point to the next were forced, with no self-awareness:

*Oedipus doesn't see that it was his mother all along. Speaking of not seeing, his decision to gouge out his eyeballs symbolizes his refusal to look at the past.*

*Mussolini was eventually killed and his body hung upside down, much like he turned Italy upside down.*

*The pandemic that stalks us in the 21st century may not be as deadly as the plague of 1347, but is nonetheless a plague to small business owners.*

Writing as Leslie allowed me to have some fun in camouflaging my own voice, but in between the flourishes, the writing had to be mostly anodyne without sounding too manufactured, with occasional slang or vocabulary culled from the class discussion boards. My clients granted me access to the boards so that I could pick up on the professors' favorite jargon and their preferred viewpoints, because Leslie would never challenge the conventional wisdom of the course.

Since I no longer arranged personal meetings, I was able to branch out nationwide while never having to post on any website beyond my initial ad in our local Craigslist. Online word of mouth sufficed. I started to cultivate my reputation for excellence rather than volume, charging a bit more per word and page, and narrowed my specialization to thesis projects.

I retired Leslie and incorporated the personalization pitch. I was lucky to learn about the development of Large Language Models in Artificial Intelligence before the general public because someone hired me to write their thesis on it. That was one of my favorite papers. I felt like a spy gathering intelligence behind enemy lines. I continued to keep an eye on its emergence out of fascination rather than fear, and to stay ahead of the curve.

No subject was off limits. I was willing to incorporate complex math into a job as long as the customer sent me the equations involved. Such papers were a lucrative vein to tap, as many of my fellow ghostwriters weren't comfortable straying too far from their discipline, and most of those disciplines were in the Humanities.

The ecotourism project was a comfortable crossover given my previous dabbles. My disabled client who liked to talk on the phone was an Environmental Science major, possibly the least sciencey of the sciences, and the way he framed his thesis drew the subject even farther out of the scientific weeds.

He was right. The travel was fun. It didn't feel like research, and I like research. This was better.

The whale watching was the best trip of them all. The four other people and I on the shuttle bus from San Diego flew out of Tijuana on a six-seat Beechcraft Bonanza. We flew high enough to see the Pacific Ocean on one side of the peninsula and the Sea of Cortez on the other, but low enough to see details in the toothy mountains and tiny towns.

A landing strip on a stretch of desert next to the lagoon surrounded in the distance by red rock formations layered like sheet cakes, a one-room corrugated metal shack of an airport with an outhouse and a weathered wind sock flapping from a pole between them, a secondhand yellow school bus with gray whales painted along its sides that rumbled toward us in a cloud of dust to pick us up, a camp of white burlap tents quivering in the wind, an army surplus mess tent rising from their midst, it all had me feeling important and forgotten, each sense alternating with the other by the second.

And that was before I had seen a single whale. I had seen bonobos in the Congo and they were fascinating, but the trip was so strenuous that it was hard to appreciate the genetic parallels we share with them while being so miserably aware of how unequipped we are to exist in their world. The boat tour of the Great Pacific Garbage Patch was an easier ride, but not much to look at: tattered shards and fragments dispersed in swirling pockets, no longer traceable to whatever flotsam they came from, rather than an island fit for dumpster diving, as I imagined it.

Whale watching combined ease of access with awe. We set out in small fishing boats with room for six, helmed by locals who could not fish the lagoon during tourist season. The whales went about their business of raising calves and resting up for the trip north as though we weren't there. We often held still, drifting with the tide, the low rumble of our idling engine interrupted by the sound of whales exhaling as they surfaced, their backs gliding under the mist formed by the air blowing through the water on their skin. When they were close enough, I liked hearing them inhale before they submerged, which sounded more human than the exhale, like someone about to see how long they could hold their breath under water in a pool. And as exciting as it was to make eye contact with one as they emerged, I also enjoyed leaning over the side to watch them disappear into the depths, their fluke fading from sight after several seconds. The water would swirl to mark the occasion, then flatten, the moment gone. They were there, right where I was looking, but I couldn't see them.

We drove into their territory for ninety minutes in the morning, and ninety minutes in the afternoon. I spent the break between voyages sitting in a chair outside my tent, its heavy burlap rustling in the sunlit breeze while I took notes for my client's thesis, feeling for an instant like an emissary to the crown, writing letters to the royal academy about what I was discovering. I put work aside for breakfast and dinner in the mess tent, conversing with the others on the tour, those I had flown with, those who were already in camp when we arrived, and those who landed after us. I made up stories about who I was and what I was doing there, practicing for when I went back to making up stories for web consumption.

The wind rarely stopped while we were there. When it did, the silence was profound. One morning before the sun came up, it finally died down after making sleep difficult for most the night. Rather than the sound of the tent being whipped, I heard whales out on the lagoon. I crawled out of my cot in the dark and found the zipper to the front door. There was just enough light outside to find my way to the bluff above the shore. I made out white puffs of spray in the distance that were slightly ahead of their sound that reached land a beat later. I heard the explosive exhales and the deep inhales, as though the earth itself was breathing.

I would have written that paper for free.

I did not write that paper for free, of course.

The voice on the phone followed through on his promise.

I made more money on that paper than any that came before. If I include travel expenses, the bill was about what I would have made if I sold my first-edition copy of *The Stranger* to that fop in the coffee house. It was enough for a down payment on a condo in a college town along a tree-lined street fit for relaxing walks in late summer and early fall. Enough to get back in the ghostwriting business on my own very selective terms. Enough to subsidize my impersonations of a journalist.

I almost sent the voice on the phone a thank-you card. I found one in the Dollar Store that would have been perfect, featuring a tree rather than flowers, and blank space inside rather than a trite stab at poetry. I held it in my hand and considered a few words of gratitude before shivering with reality and sliding it back into the display.

That's not the way this business works, I reminded myself. We don't thank each other. We fulfill obligations.

*III: Commerce, Influence, and Authorship in the Age of Self-Promotion*

With so many former clients graduated into the workforce, I eventually attracted some corporate accounts. About half the jobs I agreed to after my return to ghostwriting involved earnings and shareholder reports.

It had been a year since my globetrotting, and was beginning to wonder if it really happened, or had been a fantasy, a literal dream job. A particularly dreary contract had me speculating whether I could afford to hold out exclusively for projects that required travel and field research. It was a sales forecast for a reputable company that tapped a disreputable manager to write the summary of a month's worth of research that had already been conducted by the time he called. He had fed the data in to a variety of LLMs, but didn't know how to command the technology to give him what he wanted. I did. It was easy work, but hard to care about for more than fifteen minutes at a time.

During breaks I hacked away at an article for *The Grain*, a new venture from the editor who decided it might be worthwhile to invent a purely online source, not associated with a city, in which every article was legitimate news except one.

I was honored to be the author of the one. It concerned the production of surgical masks, and how COVID-19 was not a Chinese plot after all, but a Muslim one, designed to scare women into covering their faces, which was the first step toward Sharia law. The reporter I portrayed discovered that one of the largest shareholders of a company manufacturing N95 masks was a devout Muslim, and from there my character proceeded to fit some other circumstantial pieces together to build a plot device our readers could use in the drama inside their heads. The plot of every episode was the same: they recognize something only a select few can see. All we had to do was feed fresh details into the story arc.

Toggling between the drudgery of the corporate summary and the absurdity of the conspiracy eventually required a break from both. I scrolled YouTube for recommendations, and hovered upon an interview from a late-night talk show, which appeared in my queue thanks to having viewed clips from the show before, and having researched the topic that the celebrity guest was discussing: ecotourism.

I didn't recognize the guest, neither his name nor his image on the screen capture, which was nothing new. Since most of my time was spent conducting research and writing as someone else, a celebrity had to reach a rarified level of stardom before I would hear of them. I almost didn't click on the clip, but was curious if my old client had followed through on his boast about having connections that would lead to an audience for his thesis. Perhaps this celebrity guest was one of those connections. Maybe this actor, or singer, or whatever he was, was a friend of my client's, or an acquaintance, or whatever they call the next degree of separation in the entertainment industry.

He was none of those things.

He was my client, the voice on the phone.

I realized it before I even heard his voice. The host of the show introduced him as a child star who had gone to college to study Environmental Science, and emerged as a respected authority on the subject thanks to a highly-regarded paper he had written.

I projected myself into a science fiction tale where I watch him enter, and he is me.

He didn't make an entrance. The camera pulled back and he was already seated on the sofa next to the desk where the host held court.

I recognized the major moves that frame the paper. When he made one of those moves, I predicted which line he would paraphrase to summarize the point. I don't remember much of any other paper I wrote. His job was special. There was the line about exotic habitats being nice places to visit, but we shouldn't want to live there. There was the one about going our separate ways after we've had an encounter with the wild, based on my trip to the Philippines to swim with whale sharks in Donsol Bay.

"The whale shark keeps swimming into the distance," he recited. "We will never see that same shark again. She doesn't swim in a circle. We can't stand in front of the glass at an aquarium eating onion rings, waiting for her to come back around. We have to meet them where they are, feel how unnatural it is for us to be there. It's fun, it's exhilarating, but it's more effort than we can sustain. And we should be very suspicious of attempts to make it easier for us to be in their territory."

I didn't write "eating onion rings". I wrote "inhaling curly fries". Otherwise, his reading was verbatim.

The host looked impressed, and nodded with raised eyebrows before lowering his voice for the next question.

"People may remember you were born without the use of your legs," he gently prefaced his next question. "How did you work around that in conducting your research?"

He mentioned the research assistant. My adrenalin spiked.

"So you weren't able to go on some of these trips," the host confirmed.

"They're not exactly ADA compliant."

This inspired some overcompensating laughter from the audience.

"But then none of the places I focus on are in America," he continued. "So they don't have to worry about the Americans with Disabilities Act."

The laughter grew louder.

His research assistant faded into the distance, like a whale shark in the open sea.

The host revisited my client's childhood. His mother was a popular mommy blogger. He was featured prominently in her posts, then on the reality series it spawned. The host complimented him on finding such a productive way to deal with being cast out of the spotlight. My client pulled another line from my paper to take the compliment in stride.

"When Mobula rays jump out of the water," he appeared to ignore what the host said, "they rise several feet above the surface, flap their wings, and belly flop. We can never re-create that spectacle in captivity. We can't build the space, we can't train them. All we can do is plop them in a tank dressed up like the wild, and watch them slowly drift around. I always thought they were beautiful. I loved watching them in that self-contained field of vision. I didn't even know they could jump. Once I saw that, I was both devastated and inspired. You aren't seeing something for what it truly is unless it's free to be what it is. That's how I feel about this new phase of life. I've been let out of a tank that was dressed up like a real world, and allowed to spread my wings. And it's been humbling."

The host solemnly started to thank him. I stopped the clip before he completed the sentence.

I leaned back in my chair and let out a deep breath which probably dusted dozens of cobwebs across the ceiling.

I texted him.

"Nice interview. Let's talk. You can memorize the cadence of my voice and use that too."

No reply.

A day later I tried again with a less caustic and more sincere appeal.

I emailed.

I voice mailed.

I tried to join every one of his social media platforms and was denied.

I checked his web site for a schedule of his public appearances and found the soonest and closest.

It was in a midsize city in a midsize venue, the kind of place where a streamlined revival of an ancient Broadway musical may stop for a weekend, or on a Wednesday may host the remaining members of a band whose two hits are older than its new members. His event was half full by design, as my client's team promoted a respectful response to a recent outbreak, which had so far only inspired a recommended distancing order by the state. Being more aggressive than the government injected a sense of drama, implying the star of the show was more at risk than your average person, and also provided cover for the likelihood he couldn't fill the house for an evening that promised nothing more than presenting a slide show and answering questions. We were handed cards while we waited and told to write questions that would be considered for the Q & A session. I asked if his thesis advisor knew his work was plagiarized.

The lights dimmed until the auditorium was dark, and they didn't come back on until the audience made the move from random hoots and hollers to a slow, unified clap.

My client was already on stage when the lights popped on, sitting on a high stool behind a podium acknowledging the clapping that turned spontaneous.

His slide show featured photographs I imagined he hired someone to take. When he was done regurgitating my work, he started in on the questions that had been screened for him. Mine didn't make the cut.

For an extra forty dollars we could wait in line in the lobby for him to sign our program and pose for a selfie. I waited in the lobby, but not in line. He didn't know what I looked like, so I didn't try to catch his eye. When the crowd dwindled and I still wasn't in line, one of his handlers asked if she could help me.

"I wrote the question about the thesis advisor," I answered.

"That was a statement rather than a question," she betrayed no alarm.

"So that's why you didn't use it," I pretended to come to a realization.

"Would you like to meet him?"

"In person? Finally? Yes."

She walked behind the table where he sat winding down with the last few selfie seekers. After the last pose was struck between my client and a fan, she leaned over and spoke to him while gesturing in my direction.

He smiled and waved at me.

I didn't do anything, maybe a reflexive nod.

He backed his wheelchair away from the table and headed in my direction.

"Good to see you," he kept smiling as he came to a stop. "And when I say 'see you', I mean that literally."

"Not the greeting I was expecting," I said.

"Why?"

"Why?" his indifference amplified my surprise. "Maybe because you've been utterly unresponsive to the messages I sent."

"There was no need to respond," he shrugged. "You were violating the terms of your own agreement."

"Why so chipper now?"

"You paid to get in," his smile returned. "I'll throw in a free selfie if you'd like."

"I'd rather talk."

"We're not staying the night. We've got a gig in San Francisco day after tomorrow and I want to spend my day off there."

"You have no time to spare?"

"I've got a few minutes."

"A few minutes," I looked away and breathed slowly through my nose. "Fine. I'll take them."

"Would you please squat down or take a knee? I don't like it when people tower over me."

I obliged by squatting, grunting all the way down.

"While we're on the subject of accommodations," I said as my grunt faded. "Why are you so worried about people seeing your disability? You're already sitting next to the host on that show, you're already on stage when the lights come up tonight. You're like FDR. I thought we've come a long way since then."

"I suppose we have, especially according to those who are able-bodied."

"You once told me you've had your whole life to come to grips with it."

"Forgive me if I prefer to enjoy the thunderous applause rather than have it as background noise while I haul myself into the spotlight."

"I'd hardly describe that applause as thunderous."

"Some nights it is," he rushed past my jab. "Is this really what you wanted to talk to me about? I suspect it's not, and you've got two more minutes."

I could squat no longer. I put my knee down.

"This is way beyond what anyone has done with my work."

"The contract, that you designed, says nothing about publication."

"Given the kind of writing I produce, it never occurred to me."

"Now it has. Update your contract. Thank you for coming. You want that selfie?"

I stood up.

"I want more than that."

"I know what you're thinking," he said. "Go ahead. Publish something that blows the lid off our agreement."

He seemed clairvoyant for a moment, until I realized we had already established my lack of legal recourse.

"It won't work," he continued. "You'll never get enough people on your side."

"My side?"

"Yes."

"My side is the truth," I nearly thrust a finger into the air.

"Between us. But not in public."

I looked around to gather my thoughts. His handler kept an eye on us while some crew members broke down the table.

"You're admitting you're wrong," I said. "And admitting you won't admit it."

"Work for me instead."

"You're very good at keeping a person off-balance."

"This isn't a strategy. I mean it. I need a book to keep up the momentum."

"I'm doing fine."

"You're jealous."

"I want some credit," I acknowledged.

"You'll get it. Behind the scenes."

His handler called his name. He gestured that he would be there soon enough.

"You see now I wasn't kidding about my connections. If I let you in the circle, you're set for life. The work will be just as plentiful and ten times more lucrative than what you have going on."

I couldn't help but consider the possibility.

"Not everyone is meant to be in the spotlight," he added. "And most people who spend time in it come to find that being a kingmaker is better than being a king."

I held my pause, but no longer to consider his offer.

"I'd be a kingmaker?"

He nodded, still assured of his place in our conversation.

"What are you the king of?" I switched places with him, finally feeling on top of our exchange.

He spun around and headed for his handler.

"You'll find out," he said over his shoulder.

I felt myself plummeting and confused as to why, since I never really was on top.

*IV: Alliances and the Perception of Truth*

Mine is not the kind of business that issues press releases.

I was interviewed every so often by journalists who wrote think pieces about the ghostwriting industry, stories meant to incite slowly shaken heads in their readership while they mutter about "this generation" and "these days". When AI elbowed its way into the foreground after all those years in the background, demand for such articles dried up as journalists assumed our cottage industry was lost in the fire. But as word spread that some of us managed to thrive in spite of the threat, interview requests started to trickle in again. I received one a week after the encounter with my client.

Following a series of standard replies to the usual questions over the phone, I mentioned that not all of my clients were merely looking to get their degree over with. Some of them ended up being well-known in their field.

"I don't suppose you'd be willing to name any," she joked.

"Just one," I said.

Her pause was long, but not silent, filled with stammers and time-killers.

"Just one?" she grabbed my words and regained her footing. "You said some of them ended up being well-known in their field."

"Are you getting greedy?"

She laughed and sounded as though she was headed for another noisy pause.

"Just kidding," I put her at ease. "Being well-known in an academic field means none of your readers would know them."

"But the one..." she said with restraint and anticipation.

"The one..." I repeated with aplomb and even more aplomb.

I made her wait five seconds before saying his name.

She had never heard of him.

I was delighted to hear that.

"Plenty of people have," I testified.

I didn't know how many exactly.

After the article was published, it felt like a lot more people than I had imagined.

They were unified in their hatred of me. Their reasons varied. Some called me a snitch. Others denied I had anything to do with their hero's work. Still others didn't seem to have any reason to hate me other than they assumed their hero hated me. They contributed to comment threads with rants that made me wonder if they damaged their phones or keyboards from pounding them so hard. I vowed not to look, but started to spin adages about honesty and truth, taunted myself with accusations of weakness, then threw down a personal dare.

I sat at a café eating lunch and watched the scorn unfurl on my screen. Most of the posts adhered to a pattern: a charge of betrayal or deceit, followed by a colorful insult, which usually involved feeding a body part (usually my balls) to their exotic pet (usually an iguana). I looked up from my phone at the people around me eating and talking. Nobody knew I was being pummeled right in front of them, that hating me meant so much to so many people I had never met because of their love of someone else they had never met.

By dinner, his fan base was tired of reaching for new insults, so they started to make up stories based on information they found about people with the same name as mine. None of them discovered my side gig in fairytale journalism, thanks to my pen names, but the stories they told would have pleased my editor. They grew more exaggerated and intertwined, as though a competition was underway, where individuals arrived at the most outlandish twists and then formed teams with others who were mining similar veins, or who liked what they read and wanted in.

There was an insurance agent who shared my name, and there was an anonymous Geology major who wrote about the time he hired me to write his thesis. The fan club members decided ghostwriting was a way to distract from the drudgery of selling insurance, they made the geologist a seismologist, and then the moonlighting insurance agent used the information to hock earthquake policies.

There was a public notary with my name who was the plaintiff in a lawsuit against a riverboat casino in Indiana claiming it took advantage of his wife's gambling addiction, and there was another anonymous former client who hired me to write his dissertation on Behavioral Economics. The members again decided that ghostwriting was an alter ego for an otherwise mild-mannered civil servant, the lawsuit was a ruse to learn about the tactics of the casino industry, and the crafty notary combined that knowledge with his research on human instincts to become a gambling god banned from dozens of casinos across the country.

The further they strayed from reality, the more fascinating and less frustrating they became.

By breakfast the next morning, they had created something bigger than me that could be whatever they wanted it to be. They tried putting a face to it, but there was only one picture of me on the web, about four pages deep or three dozen screen taps in most image searches, depending on who's doing the searching and what the algorithm thinks they want. I'm in a group photo of Teaching Assistants from my second Master's Program. A click on the image reveals a caption that identifies everyone in the group, from left to right. This seemed like a pretty clear stepping stone to my future career as a ghostwriter, but the fan club didn't want clarity. They wanted a sketch pad. So the poor insurance agent found his office had been egged when he arrived to work in the morning. The public notary with a decal advertising his services on the back window of his Corolla was ambushed by a fan and her camera phone as he pulled into a Jack in the Box parking lot. He could not convince her he had no idea what she was screaming about. The members lurked around home addresses they researched, ready for a more productive confrontation than the one with the notary, but none of them made their way out to my little college town. The fan club was clustered in larger cities. They still posted their videos, not wanting their stalking to go to waste, so dozens of dazed men with the same name as mine, and one woman, were fed to the thread in a stream of bouncing, blurry denials. Their reactions were analyzed closely by the members as they tried to figure out which one was lying, which one was the culprit.

When their hero fed them a video denying my involvement in his paper, that I was nothing more than a research assistant, his argument became their argument. They settled into a cohesive narrative that felt more personal than when the news first broke, back in those early hours when the rush of anger was furious but fragmented. On his signal they were now a single bellowing voice. The same accusation rolled by, one after another. Only the obscenities changed, and even then with little variation. I was a "fucking liar" or a "lying asshole". The creative erosion was disappointing. "Lying piece of shit" was the height of their ingenuity. They were no longer vying for attention, they were simply following orders. They weren't as fun to read. The next round of attacks on those who wore my name were going to be more aggressive.

For everyone's sake, I thought it best to release a statement of my own.

I shot a video, but never showed my face.

Instead I focused on a hard copy of our contract lying on the table in my breakfast nook, where the natural light was perfect, while I narrated my case.

"I could show you receipts from the trips I took as well," I said after I covered the basics of the contract, "but I'm not interested in running up the score, I only want to set the record straight. I developed this contract after years of running my business. There is no clause dedicated to widespread publication or ensuing royalties because when I drafted this contract, everyone I had worked with, over two hundred people by that point, had enough shame to prevent them from brokering in the kind of deceit I am now shedding light on. They were shameless enough to hire me, but maintained enough of a guilty conscience to keep it at that. I never imagined a person capable of this level of shamelessness. I'm more embarrassed about my naïveté than I am angry at what it enabled. Most of all, I'm sad. Sad that someone is using their platform to get away with lying, hiding behind a noble cause and the goodwill of his supporters to do whatever he wants and take no responsibility for his actions. Thank you for listening. And I do hope you really listened."

I posted it in the comment threads of his three largest fan sites under a fake account I created to gain access.

Not expecting to sway anyone on a fan site, within hours I received calls from some of the journalists who had interviewed me, which was the goal. They wanted confirmation that it was me who had posted the video, and if I had any quotes to share.

I felt like saying if someone was not persuaded by the evidence, then they were beyond unpersuadable; they were delusional. But I wanted to keep my case insult-free, provide no emotional distraction that may excuse someone from seeing something other than what was there.

For two days after the first piece exposing my side of the story was published, a movement grew in support of it. People posted comments under the article with hashtags like #believeinghost and #fansnotsheep. They tried to do likewise in the fan sites, but their comments were deleted within minutes of posting. Some of them tweeted screenshots of their contributions before they were deleted. I was hoping a website dedicated to my evidence would appear, but momentum was waning by the time the subsequent articles were published.

My client did his part to deflate the crusade by hang gliding over a pod of orcas off the Vancouver coast. Upon landing, he decreed that his fans leave me alone, and more to the point, drop the subject.

They never spoke of me again on any of his sites, except as the implied butt of oblique jokes.

"Is that really you?" someone might caption the picture of him hang gliding.

"Who wrote this?" someone else might type in sarcasm font under his latest personal tidbit about a day in the woods or in the desert.

"Cite your source!" became a meme among them.

If anyone wanted to hear about my case, soon they would have to search for it.

I checked his site daily for an opportunity to crash another appearance.

He was scheduled to appear at the opening of an art exhibit being held in a gallery half a day's drive from home. He wasn't giving any speeches or presentations, he was simply going to be there, lending his presence to the work of a wildlife and wilderness photographer whose collection was titled, "Message in a Bottle", featuring photos of discarded plastic water bottles in spectacular locations where he was surprised to find them.

The show observed some physical distancing measures in spite of the growing sloppiness around noses and mouths. He calculated an advantage in holding the line when it came to his fans, so there was a mask requirement, a security guard-enforced radius between you and anyone else other than the single guest you were allowed to bring, and a time limit.

We were branded with wrist bands colored to coordinate with our reservation times.

I had an hour to find an opening to talk with him when no one else was within ear shot.

For forty minutes I pretended to study the photographs while keeping an eye on him from angles that prevented him from seeing me. He would probably need more than a glance to recognize me with my mask on, which was basic black to avoid drawing attention, but I took no chances. I was starting to think of alternate plans for tracking him down after the show when opportunity struck. A woman who had stepped far enough inside his invisible circle to elicit warnings from security three times was finally escorted from the exhibition on her fourth offense, which created hesitation in any other potential sycophants in the crowd, so I strolled over to the edge of his space as fast as I could while trying not to appear overanxious.

He was staring at the shot in front of him. I suspected he was pretending to focus as much as I had been.

"Do you really think all these bottles are exactly where he found them?" I asked.

"Have you always been this suspicious?" he volleyed back, "or is it the product of recent events?"

"I guess I'm not as sneaky as I thought."

"Using your real name when making a reservation doesn't help."

"It's not your event."

"I asked for a list."

"I didn't think you'd take my call."

"Really?" he spun his chair to face me. His mask was made from fabric imprinted with a jungle foliage pattern. "I figured you wanted to meet in person to keep our conversation off the record. Each of us releasing our own version and letting the people decide which one speaks to them."

I was afraid we were going too fast, and the speed would raise our intensity and then the volume.

"So you get paid just to be here?" I was careful to sound in awe rather than in judgment.

He nodded and asked what I thought of the show.

"I haven't been paying attention,'" I admitted.

"Me neither," his eyes smiled above the greenery on his mask. "Too many people to talk to. I want to earn my money."

"I was too busy waiting for my chance."

"Speaking of which..." he signaled the nearest security guard, who fastened the top button of his blazer before approaching the influencer-in-residence.

"Could you please make sure my friend and I have some privacy for the next, oh, five minutes?"

"Yes, sir."

"Five minutes, then I'm back on the clock."

"You've earned it, sir."

"See?" he looked over at me while gesturing toward the guard. "There's some nuance to this kind of gig that most people don't appreciate."

I nodded and offered an extra nod of gratitude toward the guard.

When security had their backs to the wall again, and we had our own section of the floor, he took that as his cue.

"Have you considered my offer?"

"You made me an offer?"

"Last time we spoke," he said. "I asked you to work for me."

"Oh. Right. That."

"It still stands."

I opened my mouth but couldn't even make a noise, much less speak. My mask sank into the spot where the sound was supposed to come out.

"Full credit," he touted. "Excellent pay."

I blew the cloth out from between my lips.

"A public apology?" I asked.

"You don't have to do that."

My eyes took over.

"I'm kidding," he swiped his hand through the air between us.

I laughed with polite relief.

"But no," he continued. "I won't do that."

I was almost speechless again.

"Why not?" I managed to say.

"Because I don't have to."

"You do if you want me to work for you."

"Then you won't work for me," he shrugged. "Which is too bad, because it's the best way out of this."

"For you, maybe."

"For all concerned. Even my fans."

"Not mine."

"You don't have fans," he said. "You have people who think you're telling the truth."

"I am telling the truth."

"About something that isn't really important to them. They've read about it, formed an opinion, and moved on to the next story. My people are sticking around. This means a lot to them."

I took a deep breath and slowly exhaled.

He was right.

I thought of the whales swimming past our boat in the bay as I inhaled, ready to slowly submerge, diving back down through the murky water to feed.

"How do we explain what happened?" I asked.

"A misunderstanding," he spitballed. "Miscommunication. As my research assistant, you helped me write some passages, and felt I should have made that more clear. We both got a bit stubborn about the situation and dug in, took things too far. Eventually I saw your point and wanted to make it right."

"You'll apologize for a situation we invent, but not the truth."

"The ceasefire is our hook," he sped past my observation. "They'll love it. People dig enemies coming together, a handshake they never saw coming. A hug."

He held out his arms.

"I'm not there yet," I declined.

"Understandable."

I wondered how much time we had before security broke us up. Nobody appeared to be waiting their turn. The men in blazers would probably let us go on as long as that was the case, but I wasn't sure it was necessary.

"You don't have to give me an answer now," he acknowledged the pause.

"I'm observing a moment of silence for the truth," I made up an excuse.

He laughed.

"Truth isn't dead," he insisted. "If it's inspiring. That's why I chose the environment over disabled rights."

He studied me over his mask, at last answering a question I never quite asked, but once implied.

"You don't need, I'm not..." I scrambled for the right words, but gave up. I didn't want to work that hard to lie. If I couldn't have the truth I wanted, he was at least giving me the truth I wondered about.

"Talking about my struggles wasn't going to grow my fan base," he accepted my surrender. "People don't want to hear about the times I find trash in the wheelchair lifts, or how often those lifts are out of order. Those were touching moments back when I was a kid, caught on camera looking sad. But Mom was around to seize the moment and push the narrative. Nowadays I'm the one who has to say something, and that would annoy too many people. I'm not cute enough anymore. I catch fans by putting on a show of overcoming my disabilities, ignoring them, so everyone else can feel okay about ignoring them, too. They want to be inspired, not reminded."

"Maybe you can remind them in subtle ways," I started to strategize out loud how working for him might be interesting.

"If I ever decide to go there," his eyes smiled, "it'll be my own fight. Meanwhile, if you do have to reference my condition for whatever reason, it has to be along the lines of *he may be handicapped, but you wouldn't know it from the way he lives life to the fullest.* That kind of syrup."

He spoke as if our partnership was sealed.

I thought of reasons to turn him down. There was principle, there was spite. Neither paid very well, and in either case there was loneliness.

A woman appeared on the opposite end of his invisible circle. She may have already been there, and I only noticed when I was done negotiating with myself. He turned to face her, ready to turn an admirer into a fanatic.

*V: Whether Symbiotic or Parasitic Relationships Are More Conducive to Loyalty*

I don't attend many events with him. I'm usually too busy working on his next project, or writing for someone else in his world who needs some pithy posts on their blog, or some help with their biography that needs to be published before nobody cares anymore.

When I do attend, I'm not on the stage or platform with him. I'm off to the side, against a wall, holding a notebook, ready to be called on like a producer or press secretary. He'll hesitate, usually on purpose, over a question asked by someone in the audience, so that he can ask me for help in answering, and then introduce me after we have deliberated aloud in front of everyone. He'll ask if anyone has any questions for me. If they do, they're about him. I have standard answers that make us both laugh because we've heard me say them so many times. Our laughter comes across as kinship to the audience, so they laugh too.

After our banter, I lean back against the wall as everyone turns their attention back to him, and I think about the animals I've seen thanks to our relationship. I remember the dolphin who seemed to leer at our boat with caution for the half second it hopped above the water nearby, and the sand cat who looked furious that I happened to spot her while I broke away from our camp to see if watching a desert sunset could transform me in the same way so many others claim to have been altered. There were so many lessons I could have learned from any of them, and I wonder if I chose the right ones.

He always talks about freedom being better for the animals, but their freedom might be even better for the humans in charge of them. I tell him he should include stories of animals lashing out, of orcas chewing on their trainers, chimpanzees tearing apart their owners. We both know his brand is about inspiration, so he thinks I'm kidding.

Since I have researched so many of these terrible incidents, I receive articles on my news feed about the latest animal to strike back. I tell him about it, and read the highlights out loud.

Because he believes the owners had it coming, he laughs, and expects me to join him.

Sometimes I do.

# Pigs and Other Living Things
# (a short story)

Ray has known about the pigs for months. At dusk, he watches them emerge from the tree line and creep down into the vineyard. There was a time, as a kid, when he would have gone running to his Dad, tried to catch his breath while telling him about the pigs, taken him by the hand out into the vineyard to show him the damage they had done, then stood by and watched his Dad take a few dramatic moments before announcing, "We'd better do something about those bastards."

Now, decades later, Ray could not care less. He drinks a beer he is treating himself to after a long day in the fields, and watches their big black-haired bodies raid his vines. From his vantage point outside the garage, a few hundred yards away, they seem to float down the hill. An image of floating pigs makes Ray laugh for a second.

"What's so funny?" says his brother, Phil, who is walking through the garage from the back entrance.

"I didn't see you come home," answers Ray.

"You were on the tractor, had your back to me," says Phil. "Have you seen those pigs around?"

Phil only found out about the pigs a few days ago. He and his wife were jogging around the ranch with their dog early one morning and saw them drinking from the reservoir. According to Phil's wife, she and Phil were so into their jog, they wouldn't have even seen the pigs if the dog hadn't barked and scared them away before they got too close. Apparently this was a near-death experience to her, which Ray was sure she had told to several of her friends. To Phil, it was a potential problem in trying to sell the land to any prospective buyers.

Ray looks out across the fields to the hill. The pigs have reached the vineyard and are out of sight. "No," he tells Phil. "I haven't seen them."

"I was talking to a client of mine, and he told me a friend of his hunts wild pigs with a crossbow."

Phil has a brokerage firm in town, so this sounds to Ray like one of those bored rich men who grew tired of skydiving.

"I told you," says Ray. "I'm gonna hunt 'em."

"When?" Phil presses him.

"I've got a lot of things going on right now."

"Of course, Ray," Phil snorts. "Of course you do. There are crops to kill and pipes to run over..."

"I always fix it."

"...But pigs can do a lot more damage than you can. So would you please do this? Please? Unless you want to wait and do it after I've sold the place and the pissed-off buyer calls me and wonders why half the vineyard's dying."

"I won't be around to do it, then."

Ray says this as a statement of fact, nothing more; so when his words seem to change Phil's frustration to sadness, Ray is surprised. He's not used to having his words carry much meaning.

"What's wrong, Phil?"

"What am I supposed to do?"

Ray doesn't get it. "About what?"

"Am I supposed to include a clause in the contract saying that my brother gets to live in the guest house and putter around like a zombie farmer for the rest of his life?"

And just like that, Ray is once again the sad one.

"I'll do it tomorrow night, Phil."

Ray walks back into the garage and turns on the light so he can begin to work on the tractor, which needs work just about every night. Phil keeps staring out at the ranch as it slowly disappears into the night. The song of the crickets gives some volume to the silence between them. Finally, Phil walks around the outside of the garage and back towards the house. Ray waits until he hears the door shut, then stops pretending to be busy. He can't concentrate tonight.

As he walks by the main house, Ray sees Phil's wife through the kitchen window. She is standing behind Phil, rubbing his shoulders and consoling him as he sits at the kitchen table staring into a glass of red wine.

Ray reaches the guest house and turns on the light. It is one room with a tiny kitchen jutting out from one end and a doorway leading to a connected outhouse on the other. A table stands against the far wall that Ray uses for eating and stacking mail. And above the table hangs his father's old Winchester rifle, where it has hung since the day he died.

***

"You get one shot, that's all." His Dad is giving him some last-minute advice as they lie on their stomachs on top of the pump house, waiting for the pigs. "Wait 'til they show you their eyes, then aim right between 'em."

They can see the whole ranch from on top of the shed. Everything is so healthy, so colorful. Behind them, near the front gate leading to the highway, the Christmas trees are coming in beautifully; they look like life-sized versions of the little plastic ones scattered across the hillsides of a model world built around an electric train set. To their right, the patches around the reservoir are filled with pumpkins, cut from the vines and lined up in rows; they catch the setting sunlight and glow as if they're made of neon. To their left stands the vineyard, the vines so thick that the stakes supporting them are barely visible; each row looks as though it should have some young couple posing for wedding pictures in it. Some ducks fly overhead and land in the reservoir so they can spend the night hidden in the reeds which line the shore.

"One shot," his Dad repeats the mantra.

Ray keeps on admiring the ranch as he listens to him.

"And if you miss, run like hell!"

His Dad laughs. Ray sees two pigs appear on the hill behind the vineyard. He points to them. They both fall silent. They watch them disappear behind the last row of vines, then reappear once more, coming around the corner and heading down the patch between the pumpkin patch and the vineyard. The male pig glances down each row as he passes it, as though looking for the perfect spot. With a bump and a hum, the pump turns on below Ray and his Dad. Ray flinches and yelps for a split second. The pigs turn and run. His Dad laughs.

"Look at those bastards run! Fast as cheetahs. Smart, too. You never see them freezing like a deer, wondering what to do next; no sir. Those sons o' bitches take action."

His Dad looks over and sees how distressed Ray is about scaring away the pigs. "It's an accident, kiddo. Don't worry about it. We'll get 'em tomorrow."

***

Ray drives his pickup into town the next morning. He buys fresh rounds for the gun at the sporting goods store. He also finds an excuse to visit all of the places where he does business—the heavy equipment dealer to buy a gasket for the tractor, the irrigation systems outlet for some sprinkler fittings, the hardware store for some plumber's putty—and enjoys some small talk with the owners. He's long since lost the right to have credit at each place, but they've known his family for years, and they try to give him a good deal whenever possible. The owners, and some of their employees, might even be his friends, but he prefers not to find out. He keeps the relationships transactional.

He even stops by the convalescent home to check on his mother. He doesn't see her; he just asks the nurse how she is doing. She started losing her memory during middle age, so by the time her husband was about to die and Ray brought her to his bedside to say good-bye, her last words to him were, "Do I know you?"

His father could handle it. He was grateful she said anything at all, since she rarely spoke by then.

But Ray was never able to, so the nurse tells Ray that "she's fine."

On the drive home, Ray remembers how he used to wait for that year, that grade in school, or that summer in between grades, when suddenly he would be like his Dad: always smiling, charming to everyone, at ease in any situation. But he gave up waiting a long time ago, and just got used to the tightness around his mouth, and in his stomach, and instead felt as though he was waiting for that year he started to become like his mother.

Pulling into the ranch, he notices that while clearing out this year's "Pick Your Own" pumpkin patch, he forgot to take down one of the Halloween decorations: on the edge of the vacant lot, on top of a rusted water spigot, a cardboard black cat arches its back and hisses. He closed up shop a few days ago, and he's already spent the profits in town today. If it weren't for the fact most of the customers had been coming there for years, and threw in a few extra bucks when they bought their pumpkins, he would not have even made that much. Maybe they figured out that the pumpkins were brought in from another grower's fields, since the land around the reservoir remained dormant.

Driving slowly past the dirt lot, Ray comes upon the Christmas trees. The pines he planted last year are clearly being ravaged by the same disease which hit the firs the year before last. A couple of weeks ago, he was at the drug store one morning to buy some candy for any kids who may be at the pumpkin patch later that day, and from the next aisle he heard one woman ask another woman if she knew how to get there. The prospect of some new customers made him feel good for a moment, until he heard the woman's directions:

"Oh, *that* pumpkin patch? You can't miss it. Just head up the highway for about ten miles, and it's on the right side next to the shitty Christmas trees."

If he bothered to open up for business during this holiday season, he would have about one day's worth of healthy trees. And, considering it has always been a "cut down your own tree" operation, there is no way he can buy trees from another farm and pretend they are his.

In the distance lies the vineyard. Ray can see that several of the rows are leaning to one side, the stakes collapsing with the weight of the unruly vines left to grow unchecked. It had been quite some time since any of the once-faithful wine makers had given them any business. Everyone with money seemed to realize a dream to plant a vineyard, the market boomed, and Ray couldn't get much for the grapes anymore. He had relegated the vineyard to a "pick your own" category as well, thus ending any commercial farming done on the ranch. And aside from a few gentlemen winemakers who set up operations in their garage, it turned out there was little demand for picking your own wine grapes. People would come by, sample a bite and realize they were not for eating like table grapes, and leave.

Upon entering the guest house, Ray somewhat ceremoniously removes his Dad's gun from the wall, spends the last hour before sunset cleaning it, and then heats up a can of soup for dinner. He pockets some ammunition in his jacket on his way out the door and he sees Phil waiting for him by the main house. Ray walks a little slower, trying to think of something to say in case Phil says he wants to go with him.

"Got Dad's gun out?" Phil starts talking to him before he gets there. Ray waits until he reaches him to answer.

"Yeah; fresh rounds, gave it a good cleaning."

"You want some company?"

Ray has an answer ready for him now, something he is pretty sure he heard in a move once: "Some things you've got to do alone."

Phil laughs. "It's only a pig, Ray."

All out of dramatic replies, Ray is stuck. "I just want to do it myself, Phil."

"Is this about last night? Because if it is, I'm real sorry, you know..." Phil glances at the main house. Ray follows his glance and sees Phil's wife in the window looking on. Phil continues. "...Really I am. I didn't mean to imply you're a bad farmer, not at all."

"It's okay, Phil. I am a bad farmer."

Phil looks stunned. He actually has nothing to say. And Ray, for once, is left to pick up the conversation. "I just like the grunt work; driving the tractor, moving the pipes, that stuff. I always thought you would do the other stuff."

"When have I ever shown an interest in farming, Ray?"

"No, you know...the business part of it. That's what I figured."

Phil is obviously uncomfortable with the conversation, but it's not in his nature to stop talking. "If I wasn't such a good business man, maybe I would invest in a farm. I just think they're pretty to look at."

Ray waits for Phil to continue, giving him a chance to mention their father, or their grandfather, or any of the family members who have worked the land they're now standing on, but he does not.

Phil does recognize Ray's irritation, though, and takes a stab at saying something comforting: "I'm sure whoever buys the place will need someone to take care of it."

Ray looks past Phil and sees that the sun is getting rather low on the horizon, then looks at his brother again. "All they're gonna need is someone to disc it up, so they can lease the land to some commercial growers."

"There's the vineyard, though. Everyone I've talked to loves the idea of having a vineyard on their property."

Trying to sell Ray on something puts Phil firmly back in his element. But Ray is starting to feel like this evening may actually belong to him.

"You said it yourself, Phil. It ain't like driving by on the highway and pointing out the window. It's hard; real hard." Ray turns his gaze out onto the fields, which are starting to catch the flattering light of dusk. "No more looking," he says while keeping his eyes on the expanse. "No more looking."

As he starts out toward the fields, he looks over at the window in which Phil's wife is standing and nods to her. She smiles, having no idea what was said between the two brothers. Then she looks over in Phil's direction with a slightly more quizzical expression. Ray assumes that Phil is probably shrugging and glaring at her as if to say "I tried, okay?", but he does not bother to look back and check.

Before he makes it past the Christmas trees, Ray sees two pigs floating down the hill. He reaches into his coat, grabs one of the bullets, and slides it into the rifle. Just one shot, as his Dad used to say. Behind him he hears the crackling of a car driving down the gravel road. He looks over his shoulder in time to see Phil and his wife heading for the front gate. Ray figures that Phil got all upset about their talk, and needs an expensive dinner in town to calm his nerves.

Just before reaching the other side of the reservoir, he starts to step slowly and lightly. He stops, keeping some reeds in his line of sight to the path between the original pumpkin patch and the vineyard. He leans far enough over his left foot to see down most of the path. Nothing. He walks in the same slow motion to the back of the pump house, then peers around its corner to look at the entire path. Nothing. The pigs are already down one of the rows.

Afraid of running out of daylight, he steps as quickly as he can without making any noise to the entrance of each row, then slowly lowers his head to a point where he's just able to see down each leafy aisle. As the fading light turns from orange to gray, he hears something a few rows ahead. He breathes as slowly as he can to listen closely—grunts, the rustle of vines, the rooting of dirt—then quickly skips a couple of rows and stops on one knee behind the vines which mark the entrance to the likely corridor. As he catches his breath and focuses on the world beyond his heavily beating heart, he can hear that the noises are louder. This is definitely the one.

Lowering his head just beyond the reach of the grape leaves, Ray sees the two pigs from the hillside: pitch black hair, as long and tall as a couple of hounds, but their bodies twice as thick. Their heads are buried in the base of the vine that Ray is hiding behind, about ten yards away. Suddenly a piglet scurries around from behind them, followed by two more. They stick their noses into the area where one of their parents is rooting. Apparently convinced their siblings are having more success on that side of Mom and Dad, two more come racing around to the newest hot spot, raising the total to five. Their fur is still tawny, which, along with their small size, must have helped them blend into the dry grass on the hillside and prevent Ray from seeing them earlier as they made their way down.

Ray watches them for a few moments, then raises the rifle against his shoulder. Slowly dropping his head behind the sights, Ray gently cocks the weapon. It clicks. The nearest pig raises its head in Ray's direction. Instead of looking at the pig's eyes, Ray stares at the pair of dirty white tusks which flare out of its mouth. The other pig and its piglets sense the parental alarm, and run away squealing. Ray fires, realizing a split second too late that he's not even looking through the sights anymore. He misses badly; a batch of grapes explodes on the vine above the pig. The pig doesn't even flinch and begins sprinting towards Ray. He stands up to run and the pig runs straight through his knees. With a howl, Ray falls forward as his legs are cut out from under him. He throws the gun and braces himself with his hands, landing just behind the wild pig. Ray flips himself over and sees that the tusks have cut him just below his left knee. The pig turns and clamps its mouth onto Ray's left leg just above the ankle. The pig shakes its head violently back and forth, tearing into his flesh. Ray screams in pain, beating on the pig's grunting head with his fists. With the pig showing no signs of giving up, Ray lies on his back and screams louder.

Running out of breath for a moment, Ray lets his head fall to one side and sees the rifle within reach. He grabs it and starts driving the butt into the pig's skull over and over again. Blood begins squirting into Ray's face and eyes and the pig begins to squeal. Finally he feels the pressure of the bite loosen. With another blow to the head, the pig releases him. Ray collapses onto his back once more, gasping for breath and groaning. As he stares into the purple sky, a gust of air and dust sweeps across his cheek. He turns to see that the pig has fallen next to him.

Ray stares at the pig. The pig stares straight ahead, towards the area where it had been rooting with its family just a minute ago. It struggles for breath through its smashed nose and mouth full of blood. Ray props himself up and looks down at his leg and can't tell exactly what his own situation is. His pants are torn, but there's too much blood to be able to see anything. The darkness caused by the blood is spreading across the material of his pants at a steady pace. He can't feel any pain, just warmth. He leans back, looks up at the sky, and concentrates, but still can't feel anything.

He hears the pig groaning and looks over in its direction. It shudders and moves one of its legs. Ray remembers something he had heard a few times in his life about the tribes who lived on this land for so many years, about how they'd say a prayer for any wild animal who gave their life for the greater good. Ray decides to give it a try.

"Hey," he says in the pig's direction. "Hey, pig." The pig keeps on staring straight ahead. "I just realized I don't know whether you're a male or a female. Is it the male's job to protect the family, then, or just the closest one? Well, whatever you are, I imagine you've done a pretty great thing and earned a lot of points for pig heaven, if you got one. And I'm sure all the other pigs will remember you with a lot of respect and honor, once they hear about what you did. I know if I had a family, I hope I'd protect them as good as you did. Now, I might as well tell you my brother isn't gonna eat you. He's not gonna know what to do with you. So I'm afraid you're probably gonna end up laying out here for days while he screws around looking for someone to do the dirty work for him. Maybe he'll put you on Craigslist, or something on the web. Hopefully he'll do the smart thing and get some of the field workers around here to take you home. They'll eat you. I just hope he doesn't sell you to them, as if he needs the money more than those poor bastards need a free meal. Even if you end up on the trash heap, though, or in a bonfire, I just want to tell you that you have died a useful death in the eyes of humans, if that worries you at all. I'm what's called a fuck-up. The one thing I love, I got no talent for. So I can't do anything else, and no one's gonna want me to do what I can do, since I do it so badly, so what the hell? I know that doesn't sound like much of an honor to you, getting rid of someone like me, but you're actually helping out a lot of people. Nobody's gotta feel sorry or guilty for me anymore, and the taxpayers are gonna save some money this way, too, because about all I'd be able to do is hold out my hand once this place is sold. We owe so much on it, that whatever my share is won't last me very long. So really, you're a hero. Take my word for it. You're a hero."

Ray looks down at his leg and notices the darkness is spreading a little slower now, but realizes it's probably because the blood is covering a larger area than before. "But if I make it through this and walk with a limp on top of everything else," he says to the pig, "you can rot in pig hell for all I care."

He laughs at his own joke and his extremities quiver, which loosens up the numbness and unleashes a scorching pain that slices through his nerve endings. He winces and tightens up, bracing himself against the agony. The exertion can only last so long, and he collapses onto his back and gasps for air. His head flops to one side and he spots the bullets which fell out of his pocket during the attack. He grabs one and then scans the area for his Dad's rifle. It's behind him just within reach as he stretches out as far as he can extend. Grateful for a chance to end the pain, he locks the bullet into place, but then realizes something before turning the gun on himself.

"Damn," he thinks out loud for the pig's sake. "This is all wrong. I bet getting beat to death by a human isn't real honorable for you. If you guys make it past a bullet, you're probably supposed to mop the floor with us. And on the other hand, for me to miss like that, then end up with a bullet in my head, what is that gonna look like on the morning jog tomorrow? Might as well both go out like heroes."

Ray drags himself over to the pig, screaming the entire way, and positions himself in front of the beast, making sure his battered leg is near the pig's tusks. The left leg of his pants is now almost completely darkened by blood. Ray feels light-headed, and lies on his back to take a few deep breaths. He grips the gun tightly, rises, rests the barrel between the pig's eyes, and cocks it. "In the name of the God of All Pigs, I thank you." He looks into the pig's eyes and pulls the trigger.

Lying on his back once more, Ray looks up at the sky. The darkness has spread across everything, and the stars are beginning to reveal themselves, one by one.

# Also by Sean Boling

**The Current Mr. Orr**
Devin's Best Afterlife
Once in Two Lifetimes
Revenge and Wellness in the Sweet Hereafter

**Standalone**
Cut Flowers
Abraham the Anchor Baby Terrorist
The Summer of Our Foreclosure
Satellite Campus
A Charter to That Other Place
The Latest Version of My Love Story
Show Them What They Won
The Name Field
Should
Moral Adjacent
Over Here We Have
The Current Mr. Orr

# About the Author

Sean lives with his family in Templeton, California. He teaches English at Cuesta College.